LUCKY CHARM

A SPELLBOUND PARANORMAL COZY MYSTERY, BOOK 4

ANNABEL CHASE

RED PALM PRESS LLC

Lucky Charm

A Spellbound Paranormal Cozy Mystery, Book 4

By Annabel Chase

Sign up for my newsletter here http://eepurl.com/ctYNzf and or like me on Facebook so you can find out about new releases.

Copyright © 2017 Red Palm Press LLC

All rights reserved. This book or any portion thereof may not be reproduced or used in any manner without the express written permission of the author, except for the use of brief quotations in a book review.

This is a work of fiction. Names, characters, businesses, places, events and incidents are either the products of the author's imagination or used in a fictitious manner. Any resemblance to actual persons, living or dead, or actual events is purely coincidental.

Cover Design by Alchemy

❀ Created with Vellum

CHAPTER 1

"You're going to wear that?" Gareth asked. It was impossible to miss the criticism in his tone, mainly because he made no effort to disguise it.

I looked down at my tasteful blouse and trousers. "I'm attending a funeral, Gareth. What do you expect me to wear? The dress I wore to the Spellbound High School dance?"

"Well, you might have more fun if you exposed a little flesh."

Argh. What was it with vampires and exposed flesh?

I turned to face my vampire ghost roommate. "I am attending the funeral of a wizard I've never met. I hardly think fun should be at the top of my agenda." It was also my first official coven ceremony.

"Aye. You're right. I suppose it doesn't really matter what you wear anyway," Gareth said. "Your grief cloak will cover it."

I froze. "What's a grief cloak?"

He clucked his tongue. "Have they still not told you about proper attire? Academy standards really are slipping." The academy was the Arabella St. Simon Academy, where I

1

attended remedial witchcraft classes. I was new to witchcraft—new to the town of Spellbound and all its paranormal ways—and the grief cloak was the latest on a long list of Important Things I Still Didn't Know.

"Should I send Sedgwick over to Begonia's? Or maybe to Millie's?" I knew one of my classmates would have a spare cloak. They each had older siblings and, as a result, lots of hand-me-downs.

"As long as you wear your black cloak, you'll be fine," Gareth said. "Most of the coven's grief cloaks have symbolic embroidery of some kind. You'll see later."

"I'm just glad it will be dark outside, so that I don't have to fly solo on my broom," I said. With my intense fear of heights, it was bad enough that I had to ride on a broomstick at all. The funeral, however, was to be held on Swan Lake at midnight. Part of the coven ritual. Although I had passed the first phase of broomstick training, I still wasn't permitted to ride past sunset. I needed to log more hours in the air first. Many more hours than I was willing to spend hundreds of feet above the ground with only a narrow piece of wood between my legs.

"So whose broom are you riding on?" he asked. "And do they know what to expect?"

I glared at him over my shoulder. "I took an extra dose of anti-anxiety potion after dinner. I have no intention of disgracing myself at a funeral."

Gareth chuckled. "Knowing you, I'm sure you'll find a way."

I pulled a black cloak from the back of my closet and swung it over my shoulders. "I hope it's not too chilly at the lake." The weather in town tended to stay on the mild side, despite its location near the Pocono Mountains—all thanks to the spell that contained the town and allowed creatures of the night to walk around in daylight without burning to a Kentucky Fried crisp.

"I'm riding with Ginger," I said.

"How did she draw the unlucky straw?" he asked.

I went into the bathroom to brush my hair. "I am not an unlucky straw. Ginger volunteered. She told me so herself."

Gareth stifled a laugh. "Are you certain? She has that beautiful red hair. I bet she prefers it without vomit."

Magpie screeched, alerting us to Ginger's arrival before the wind chimes clanged. I shot a quizzical look at Gareth.

"That's new," I said. "Magpie doesn't usually act like a watchdog."

Gareth shrugged. "Perhaps he's coming around to you."

Doubtful. The only thing Magpie came around for was a can of tuna and to torment me with his soul-sucking face.

I hustled downstairs to open the door for Ginger.

"Aren't you so excited?" she asked, as I opened the door. "Your first coven funeral."

"It's my first funeral in Spellbound, actually," I said. Although I'd watched the funeral procession for Gareth, I hadn't attended. The long line of vampires in red cloaks had been far too intimidating. Not to mention the fact that I hadn't met Gareth at that point. I had the distinct pleasure of making his acquaintance after he was the walking dead undead.

"Is that your only cloak?" Ginger asked, frowning.

Oh boy. "It is, but it's black and it'll be dark outside, right?"

Ginger brightened. "You're right. It'll be fine. We'll have to put it on the list for later, though. You'll definitely need a grief cloak. Everyone in the coven has one."

"Told you so," Gareth called after me.

I stuck out my tongue before following Ginger out the door. Her broomstick was in the driveway, propped up against my 1988 green Volvo, affectionately known as Sigmund.

"You sure you're ready to fly with me at night?" Ginger asked.

"Do I have a choice?"

The sky was black as we rode through the chilly night air with only the moon's light to guide us. Ginger made sure to position me in front of her, just in case my anti-anxiety potion failed me. The fey lanterns of Spellbound twinkled below. I tried my best to enjoy the moment, even though I was scared witless. My fingers ached from the tight grip I had on the broom handle. I was relieved when we arrived on the shores of Swan Lake. It looked so different from my first encounter. It had been daylight when I got lost in my car and ended up on the other side of the lake. The day my life was forever altered.

Tonight the shore was dotted with black cloaks. I noticed the floating funeral pyre and quickly realized what kind of ritual this was going to be.

"We're going to burn him?" I asked.

Ginger looked at me like I had two heads. "Of course. What did you expect?"

So we were Vikings? "But Raisa was a witch and she was buried on the grounds of her cottage."

"Raisa was never one to follow Spellbound traditions. Plus, she wasn't one of us."

Technically, neither was I.

Once everyone had arrived, Lady Weatherby took her place beside the float, which was currently anchored to shore. Her long cloak billowed in the breeze. The darkness and somber occasion managed to enhance her commanding presence.

"We are gathered here to celebrate the life of Josef, a beloved wizard of Spellbound. He has walked through the doorway to the other side where our ancestors await him with open arms. May the spirits guide him and may he find everlasting peace."

"The winds in the East rise for you, Josef," a group of witches cried.

"The winds of the West will steer you to everlasting peace," another group cried.

"Josef's son, Felix will do the honors." A middle-aged man stood beside Lady Weatherby, clutching a thick wooden stick. He extended it toward her and, with the flick of her fingers, flames sprouted from the wood. He walked over and the flames kissed the floating pyre. They began to lick the wood, slowly at first and then quite greedily. The anchor was removed and the wooden structure floated toward the middle of the lake. The fire burned hotter and brighter, cutting a striking image on the darkened body of water. Everyone on the shore joined hands and began to sing. Unsurprisingly, I didn't recognize the song. It was a haunting melody, sad yet strangely uplifting.

As atmospheric as the whole ritual was, I was relieved when it was finally over. Funerals made me uneasy given my history. I'd attended my mother's when I was three and my father's when I was seven. My father's parents followed later.

Dozens of broomsticks launched into the air at once and I was amazed that there were no accidents. Unlike me, the rest of the coven seemed to know what they were doing. We flew back to town, where everyone gathered for refreshments in the all-purpose room of the academy.

"He looked good for a three-day wake," someone commented. Because the coven waited for the full moon to perform the ritual, the body was laid out for three days in Josef's house. I didn't attend the wake, but it seemed that everyone was relieved it wasn't a twenty-day wake. Those were apparently brutal. And smelly.

I waited in line to offer my condolences to Felix. This was the hardest part for me, being confronted with someone else's pain. It hit too close to home.

"Emma Hart, isn't it?" Felix said, shaking my hand. He was average height with a slim build and kind eyes.

"Yes, it's nice to meet you. I wish we were meeting under happier circumstances."

"Death comes for all of us eventually, I'm afraid," he said. "It was my father's time and he knew it. He was well prepared and, oddly, that is a comfort."

"It's not odd at all," I said. Although I was still young when my grandmother died, her death didn't come as a shock like the others. We'd had a little time to prepare and that somehow made her passing easier.

"This is your first ritual, I hear," Felix said. "I'm sorry to make it a funeral."

"No, it was amazing," I said. "Very moving."

"Speaking of moving," a voice said behind me. "Let's get on with it."

I looked behind me to see Jemima, a young witch with a sour attitude. I'd tried to befriend her, but her personality didn't make it easy.

"It was good to meet you, Felix," I said.

"Same here."

I found Ginger standing next to the refreshment table, chatting with her sister and a few of the older members of the coven.

"What did you think?" she asked, handing me a cup of burstberry juice.

"It was breathtaking," I said. "What happens to the floating funeral pyre?" I knew firsthand that the magical border of Spellbound extended partway into the lake. I wasn't sure if Josef's float would simply bounce off the invisible barrier and eventually drift back to shore.

"We do a spell that allows it to disintegrate by sunrise," Ginger said.

Magically efficient.

"No one seems sad," I said. "Did Josef have friends in the coven?"

"He kept to himself in his later years," Ginger said, "but he had friends. Josef was a huge advocate for animal rights, too. He donated a lot of money to Paws and Claws over the years."

I had a certain fondness for the animal rescue center since that was where I met Sedgwick.

"Death for someone like Josef isn't a sad ending," Meg interjected. Ginger's older sister shared her flaming red hair and alabaster skin. "It's simply a new beginning."

Was that how Gareth saw his latest incarnation as a vampire ghost? A new beginning? I guess it was one way of looking on the bright side.

"How long will people stay here?" I asked, fighting the yawn that was building inside of me.

"Until sunrise," Ginger replied, and I nearly spit my burstberry juice all over her grief cloak.

"Not everyone," Meg added quickly, gauging my reaction. "Only those who want to and can. We know you have class in the morning."

I gulped down the remainder of my juice. I was a functional insomniac. I'd give it my best shot.

CHAPTER 2

On the way to class the next morning, I snagged a latte from Brew-Ha-Ha with an extra shot of 'bright eyed and bushy tailed.' Everyone in the classroom seemed to be struggling to stay awake. Ginger basically phoned in a lesson on witches and their relationship to nature. Each time she mentioned the earth or the ground, I pictured myself curling up in a ball in the grass outside and falling asleep. So much for the potency of my extra shot.

By the end of the class, I was openly yawning, but I didn't worry because so was everyone else, including Ginger. I got the impression that she continued socializing somewhere else after she dropped me at home.

A white-faced owl swooped into the room, grazing the top of Sophie's head. Good thing she was resting it on the table. A spot of drool glistened in the sunlight.

The owl dropped a message on the desk in front of Ginger and flew straight out the door without stopping. Ginger unrolled the note.

"Emma, Lady Weatherby and Professor Holmes would like to see you in her office after class."

Uh oh. That's not a message any witch wants to receive.

Begonia's brow creased with worry. "What do you think they want?"

I had my suspicions, but I'd wait until the conversation actually took place to confirm them.

"I'm sure it's nothing," I said. "Lady Weatherby probably just wants to tell me that my grip on my wand is too loose or something. She's always on my case to practice."

I left the classroom and walked down several long corridors until I reached Lady Weatherby's office at the far end of the building. It was the largest office in the building, as one would expect. On the wall behind her desk hung a portrait of a young and vibrant witch. She wore the very same headdress of twisted antlers that Lady Weatherby wore now.

"Who is that?" I asked, pointing to the portrait.

Lady Weatherby clasped her hands together. "I'm glad you asked. She is Arabella St. Simon. The academy's namesake."

So she was the one we had to thank for the ASS Academy? Nice going, Arabella.

"She looks so young," I said. And yet she was wearing the headdress that indicated she'd been the head of the coven. How long ago was that? Lady Weatherby was the current head and before her was her mother, Agnes.

"Arabella was the youngest head of the coven in our history," she said. "She was greatly revered, hence the academy."

Professor Holmes sat in the chair closest to the desk. He gestured for me to sit beside him.

"So what's her story?" I asked. I figured she must be deceased by now.

"She was the strongest head of the coven in a thousand years," Lady Weatherby said, with more emotion than she generally mustered. "Her death was a tragedy and we mourn her loss to this day. It is an honor for me to sit beneath her watchful gaze every day. It makes me aspire to do great things."

So Lady Weatherby admired Arabella greatly, but had a tumultuous relationship with her own mother. I wondered what the difference was between Arabella and Agnes.

Over in the corner, a black cat awoke from a nap. There was so much hair that I could scarcely discern its face from its bottom. Only when it raised its head did I realize that the cat wore a tiny headdress identical to Lady Weatherby's. I squelched my laughter, not wanting to insult anyone.

Lady Weatherby followed my gaze to the stretching cat. Magpie would kill for some of that fluff.

"That is Chairman Meow," Lady Weatherby said. "My familiar. You do remember that the rest of us have feline familiars here."

Although I'd seen Lady Weatherby's familiar in passing, this was the closest I'd ever been to him. He tended to keep a respectful distance.

"He has beautiful green eyes," I said. They shone so brightly that I had no doubt they glowed in the dark. "Does he mind wearing the headdress?"

When I was nine, I remembered my neighbor trying to coax his dog into wearing reindeer antlers for Christmas. It didn't end well for the antlers. Chairman Meow struck me as the type of cat that would speak his mind if displeased. In fact, I suspected that he and Magpie would get along swimmingly.

"He does not mind the headdress," Lady Weatherby said. "Now if we can please get back to business. Professor Holmes tells me that you were able to communicate with Raisa at her cottage. He further informed me that you were unaware that you were dealing with a ghost." She tapped her fingernails on the desk in a gesture that was reminiscent of her mother. Agnes tapped her own twisted fingernails in a similar fashion when I visited her in the Spellbound Care Home. I had a feeling Lady Weatherby wouldn't appreciate the comparison.

"She was different from Gareth," I explained. "She could touch things, move things. She made me a drink called Pure of Heart." And she frightened the living daylights out of me.

Lady Weatherby and Professor Holmes exchanged a look.

"So she neglected to tell you that she had passed on?" Lady Weatherby asked.

"I only found out the truth when I ran into Professor Holmes on the way back home." It had been quite a shock to discover she was dead. The old witch even had iron teeth. The sound of their clicking had haunted my dreams ever since that day.

"We have been assuming that your ability to see Gareth was the result of his connection to his former house and office. Now we are not so certain." Lady Weatherby's expression was a mixture of concern and frustration.

"I have no connection to Raisa," I said. "She told me herself that we weren't part of the same coven. She knew about my birthmark, though."

Lady Weatherby's brow lifted. "Birthmark? What birthmark?"

Oops. Probably should have reported that discovery. "I have a small birthmark on the nape of my neck in the shape of a little blue star. Raisa seemed to know about it even though I was unaware of it."

Professor Holmes stood and walked to the back of my chair. "May we see it?"

I lifted my hair off my neck and displayed the birthmark. He studied it for a moment before beckoning Lady Weatherby over. Wordlessly, she rose from her chair and stood behind me.

"Fascinating," she said. "It is very much like a star."

"And blue at that," Professor Holmes added.

"What do you think it means?" I asked. "Raisa seemed to know I was coming, too. And she knew Sedgwick's name."

Lady Weatherby returned to her seat behind the desk. "She is beyond the veil now. She has access to more information than you and I could dream of."

"Then why couldn't she tell me about my coven? She didn't seem to have all of the answers."

"No, death does not make us omniscient," Lady Weatherby replied. "However, she is infinitely wiser now than she was when she was living."

"Like Gandalf when he levels up from a grey wizard to a white one," I said.

Lady Weatherby stared down her aquiline nose at me. "Your human references have no relevance here."

I begged to differ. "Do you think it's worth going to see her again?" Although I didn't love the idea of revisiting the creepy cottage with the boneyard, I'd suck it up if it meant answers.

"No," Lady Weatherby and Professor Holmes said in unison.

"Raisa is dangerous," Professor Holmes said. "Living or dead."

"I shall have members of the coven research the birthmark," Lady Weatherby said. "Thank you for your candor. I expect you will alert us to any further discoveries."

I nodded. "I'm as eager to know more about myself as you are." I meant it. I wanted to learn more about my mother and her side of the family. Did she know she was a witch? What happened to her parents? Was her death an accident?

"I've been meaning to tell you," Lady Weatherby said, as I rose to my feet. "I tried your Magically Delicious Muffins. Your baking is not as terrible as I expected."

It was the closest she would come to a compliment.

"Um, thank you?"

To my surprise, Chairman Meow escorted me to the door. He had a regal air about him and I could only assume that came from his position as Lady Weatherby's familiar. From his purposeful strides, I couldn't decide whether he was politely seeing me out or throwing me out. When it came to cats, it was hard to tell.

Millie stood on my doorstep, arms crossed and a scowl on her face.

"Hey Millie," I said. "What's going on?"

She blew straight past me and into the house. "They revoked my broomstick license for a whole month," she complained.

I couldn't hide my surprise. Millie was the star pupil in our broomstick flying class. "How did that happen?"

"Do you have anything to drink?" she asked. "I had to walk all the way here and now I'm parched."

"Sure," I said, gesturing for her to follow me into the kitchen.

"Do you have any zazzle punch?" she asked. "That's my favorite."

"I'm afraid I don't. How about lime fizz?"

She groaned. "I suppose that will have to do."

I poured her a glass of lime fizz and we settled down at the counter.

"So what happened? You fly a broomstick as well as any witch in the coven."

Millie couldn't resist a proud smile. "I was late coming home from the hideout last night," she said. "I was in danger of missing my curfew, so I decided to fly home." Millie's broomstick license, like mine, was provisional. We were only permitted to fly during daylight hours until we passed the next phase.

"You flew in the dark?"

"The sun had only just set," she said bitterly. "It was my stupid luck that Sheriff Hugo was out on the golf course at the country club and saw me fly overhead."

"And he recognized you?"

"Of course." She guzzled down her lime fizz. "I never should've stayed for the end of the movie. I ended up missing curfew and losing my license. So not worth it."

I resisted the urge to tell her that rules existed for a reason. That didn't seem like the kind of response he was looking for. Then again, I was surprised she would come to me at all. Although we were friends, we weren't as close as she and Sophie.

"I was wondering if you might have any way of helping me get my license back," Millie said.

Now I understood. She wasn't here for sympathy. She was here for action.

"I'm a public defender, Millie," I said. "I don't have any involvement in the bureaucratic end of things."

Millie ran her index finger along the rim of the glass. "But people seem to listen to you. Maybe you could just lay out my case."

"It's only a month, Millie. If I were you, I would just wait it out."

Millie's face reddened. "That's because you don't like to fly. It's going to be torture for me to not have my broomstick for an entire month. Why do we even have all these stupid rules?"

"I'm really sorry. I wish I could help."

Millie's shoulders slumped. "I suppose I can just ride tandem for the rest of the month. At least that would allow me time in the air, although it won't count toward my full license."

Magpie wandered in, took one look at Millie, and hissed before scampering into an adjacent room.

"I've been thinking," Millie said, eyeing the empty doorway. "This cat of yours might improve his behavior if he spent more time around other cats."

"What exactly are you proposing? A party?" I bit back a laugh at the thought of cats sitting around the table in party hats.

"Something like that," she said, completely serious. "Our familiars tend to spend a lot of time together. It wouldn't be out of the question to include Magpie, even though he isn't your familiar."

I was touched. Millie wasn't the warmest witch in Spellbound, but her idea was a thoughtful one.

"I can't say for certain that Magpie will go along with it, but I'm certainly willing to try." I'd say the hairless cat was grumpy ever since his owner died, except I had the sense that Magpie's personality was unchanged by Gareth's death.

Millie clapped her hands. "Well, this cheers me up, despite the pesky license situation. I'll speak to the other girls and we'll arrange something."

"It's probably best if I host," I said. "I don't know how amenable Magpie would be to leaving the house." I glanced down at the savage beast, as he studied Millie with his usual murderous eyes.

Millie took a nervous step backward. "Yes, here is probably best. Where his owner can keep him in line."

"Magpie doesn't really have an owner now," I said. If he ever truly did.

"Well, hopefully we can work on smoothing his rough edges."

Rough edges was putting it mildly. "If he doesn't draw blood, I'll consider the party a success."

Millie scrunched up her nose. "You and I have vastly different definitions of success."

Given that my measure of success was not puking during flight on a broomstick and Millie's was executing a perfect ninety-degree angle, she wasn't wrong.

"I'm sure we do, Millie. I'm sure we do."

CHAPTER 3

Today was the day I'd designated to see the town council about organizing a commission to review Spellbound's sentencing guidelines. Traditionally, crimes were firmly punished here, but it had recently come to light that many residents felt the length of sentences was too harsh. Certain people, including prosecuting attorney Rochester, felt that it was time to take a closer look at Spellbound's laws and see whether changes could and should be made. Thanks to my fairy friend Lucy, who served as the assistant to Mayor Knightsbridge, I knew that the council was meeting at ten. I wore my most professional-looking outfit and took extra time with my hair, much to Gareth's relief. I wanted my proposal to be taken seriously, so I needed to look the part.

I ran into Lucy in front of the Great Hall. She was busy shooing pigeons away from the overhang above the entrance.

"There you are," she said, fluttering toward me. Her pink wings glistened in the sunlight.

"Have they started yet?" I asked, as we entered the building.

"No, you've arrived just in time."

Lucy looped her arm through mine and steered me toward the double doors that led into the Great Hall.

The Great Hall was an impressive structure. From its high ceilings and stunning architecture to its grand lobby, it was the right place to make big decisions. My trials were also held here, so I was starting to know the building well. Although my office was close by, I wasn't fortunate enough to be in the same building. That honor was reserved for the registrar's office, the very first place I'd ever visited in Spellbound.

"They won't mind, will they?" I asked. "You said residents show up unannounced all the time at these meetings, right?"

Lucy chewed her lip. "I wouldn't say all the time. Just because they're allowed to come during open meetings doesn't mean they feel encouraged to do so."

"What determines whether a meeting is open or closed?"

"It depends on what's on the agenda. If they're making important decisions, they'll sometimes ask for feedback in advance and consider the issue behind closed doors. Today is listed as an open meeting."

"And you'll tell me when it's the right time for me to speak?" I asked.

"You can count on me."

Lucy pushed open the double doors and froze beside me. I didn't realize what the problem was until I saw the council members. Wayne Stone, part-time accountant and full-time troll, was in the process of jumping down from the dais to the floor below.

"What's he doing?" I asked in a hushed tone. "He's going to hurt himself." Trolls did not get much stockier than Wayne. He was liable to give himself a hernia or blow out a knee.

"It isn't just Wayne," Lucy said, her eyes round. "Check out Lord Gilder."

Oh my. Lord Gilder, head of the vampire coven and an

incredibly formal member of the council, was balancing his gavel on the tip of his nose like a circus seal. The elegant yet fearsome Lady Weatherby sat beside him, clapping merrily at his performance.

"Something is terribly wrong," Lucy said.

To the untrained eye, it simply appeared that the town council was letting loose for change. We knew better. The council never loosened up.

Lucy gasped. "Did you see that? Lady Weatherby just did a cartwheel and her cloak blew up in the process." She covered her mouth. "Her underpants are black lace. I can't unsee that!"

"Stop right there," I insisted. I didn't want any more details. "They're acting like children."

"Stars and stones, it must be a spell," Lucy said.

A spell on the entire town council. Egads. "What do we do?"

"Well, one of my former jobs was running a preschool. Let's see if I still have the skills." Lucy fluttered forward, snapping her fingers. "One, two, three. All eyes on me." The members of the council stopped what they were doing and stared at the dark-haired fairy. Lucy glanced at me over her shoulder and winked.

"You're not the boss of me," Maeve McCullen said. Maeve was a banshee and the owner of the town theatre. She was as theatrical as she was pretty. For a brief moment, I wondered whether this was all an act. Then Lorenzo Mancini jumped on top of one of the tables and howled like the moon was shining directly in his face. Not typical behavior for the reserved alpha of the werewolf pack.

"Now what?" Lucy whispered.

"Please have a seat," I said. "We need everyone to be calm and quiet." I tried desperately to remember all of the phrases my grandparents had used to quiet me when I was small. I had no experience in dealing with children other than the fact that I'd once been one.

From out of nowhere, a snowball hit me in the face. My cheek burned from the cold. I heard giggling from the dais.

"Okay," I yelled. "Who did that?"

Everyone remained silent. Since it was an indoor snowball in sixty-degree weather, it had to be someone with access to magic, which narrowed down the pool of suspects.

"Lady Weatherby did it," Juliet piped up. The statuesque Amazon sat quietly in her chair, sucking her thumb.

Lady Weatherby jerked her head toward Juliet. "You always were a crybaby," she accused.

"And you've always been a bully," Juliet shot back.

Oh dear. This could get ugly fast if we didn't get it under control. Some of these council members packed a serious magical punch. If they weren't in a mature frame of mind, who knew what the repercussions would be?

"I think I'd better go get Sheriff Hugo," Lucy said.

"Really?" I asked. The sheriff wasn't exactly known for his diligent efforts in the area of law enforcement.

"Do you have any better suggestions?"

I didn't. "Do you know a spell that can contain them while I wait?" I didn't want all hell to break loose while I was alone with the council members.

Before she could answer, the double doors burst open and an elf came riding in on a unicycle. It was Stan, the registrar.

"What on earth?" Lucy exclaimed.

The room erupted at the sight of the unicycle.

"I want a turn," Maeve called.

"Me first," Wayne said. He advanced toward the elf until I whipped out my wand, Tiffany.

"Nobody move a muscle," I said. "I have a wand and I'm not afraid to use it."

Big mistake. Lady Weatherby pulled out her more impressive wand. "I have one too. Let's see whose is better."

"No, no, no," Lucy whispered.

"Lucy, hurry and get Sheriff Hugo. I'm going to need help keeping them still." Literally. They were all bouncing around like they needed the toilet.

"I'll be back in a jiffy," Lucy promised. I seriously hoped a jiffy meant teleportation. Even five minutes would be too long with this crew.

Stan hopped off his unicycle and sat down in a nearby chair. "Is this a playgroup? I was bored in my office all by myself."

"Let's play Magic and Mayhem," Mayor Knightsbridge cried.

The word 'mayhem' in the title suggested that was not a good idea. I racked my brain for a spell I could use to keep them from getting out of hand.

Then I remembered the Sleeping Beauty spell.

The Sleeping Beauty spell was a basic defensive spell that Lady Weatherby had taught me. It was ironic that I was about to use it on her. I knew the spell wouldn't last long, but it would give me enough time to get help. If they were anything like the kids I knew, they were going to be full of energy when they woke up. I was definitely going to need backup.

I focused my will, held out my wand, and said, "I'm in too deep/please go to sleep."

I hurried out of the Great Hall and secured the double doors behind me. I needed to find someone from the coven. Quickly.

Professor Holmes and I entered the Great Hall to the sound of gentle snoring. Lorenzo was just stirring. Perfect timing.

The elderly wizard's eyebrow quirked. "Children, you say? I see a bunch of old timers taking their morning nap."

"Just wait," I said.

"I'm hungry," Lorenzo said, and began to cry.

Professor Holmes looked at me askance. "I'm beginning to understand."

He approached the dais and stood across from Lady Weatherby as her eyes opened. She stretched her arms overhead and stifled a yawn.

"J.R., do you recognize me?" he asked.

She hunched forward and peered into his eyes. Then, quick as a flash, her hand darted out and snatched his pointy blue hat. "This looks better on me." She set it on top of her antler headdress.

"J.R., it's me. Francis. We work together."

Lady Weatherby giggled. "I know, silly. But all work and no play makes J.R. a dull girl."

I sincerely hoped she was quoting the nursery rhyme and not The Shining. With Lady Weatherby, I couldn't be too sure.

"And you have no idea what happened here?" he asked me.

I shook my head. "Lucy and I arrived in time for the meeting. I was going to present a proposal. They were like this when we came in."

"And Stan?" he asked. "Was he in here too?"

"No, he came from his office. The spell must have impacted everyone in the building at the time." He was just collateral damage.

"Why would someone do this?" He tugged on his ear, thinking. "We need to address this promptly. We simply cannot have every member of the council acting like a child. It puts the entire town at risk."

"You're preaching to the choir," I said. "Lucy went to get

Sheriff Hugo." The fact that she hadn't returned yet suggested that he was nowhere to be found.

"Well, we cannot keep putting them to sleep," the professor said. "We shall have to come up with some other means of keeping them safe."

"It works both ways," I said. "We need to keep residents safe from them as well." We needed to start by collecting the wands of Lady Weatherby and Mayor Knightsbridge. The magic of both the head of the coven and the powerful fairy was too potent to leave unattended.

I fished two lollipops out of my handbag. I tended to keep random snacks in there for when I was at the office and feeling hungry. I knew an apple would be better for me, but Taffy's was the best candy shop I'd ever seen and it was located right in the town square. Too tempting to avoid.

"Lady Weatherby and Mayor Knightsbridge," I called. "I'd like to trade you one of these amazing lollipops for your wands." I held out the two lollipops for inspection. The mayor's eyes popped at the sight of the sparkly pink one in my left hand.

"That one! That one!"

She snatched it from me and handed over her glittering wand. Next I did the same with Lady Weatherby. Although it didn't render them powerless, it significantly reduced the harm they were capable of.

Sheriff Hugo galloped into the Great Hall, followed by Lucy and his deputy, Astrid the Valkyrie.

"Please tell me this is a joke," the centaur said.

"I'm afraid not," Professor Holmes said gravely.

"Do we know anything about the spell?" Sheriff Hugo asked. "Is it one of those that only lasts for a limited time?"

"I'm afraid I have no idea without knowing the particulars of the spell," Professor Holmes said.

A ball whacked Sheriff Hugo in the back of the head and

he whipped around to locate the offender. Lord Gilder and Lorenzo each pointed an accusatory finger at the other.

"This is unacceptable," Sheriff Hugo muttered.

"First we need to find somewhere safe to keep the council and Stan," I said, raising my voice over the sound of screeching and laughter. "Then we can focus on finding the culprit and breaking the spell." The 'children' were so noisy when they were awake—I wondered how parents accomplished anything with kids at home.

"She pushed me," Maeve cried.

I turned around to see Maeve on the floor, wiping tears from her eyes. Mayor Knightsbridge fluttered in front of her, wearing a Cheshire Cat grin.

"She tripped," the mayor said, her eyes widening to the picture of innocence. "It was an accident."

"What did I trip on—your wing?" Maeve shot back. "My legs aren't that long. I'm not Juliet."

"Hey," Juliet objected. "Are you making fun of my height?"

I rubbed my temples. This was going to be an impossible task. "I think we should separate them. Can we divide them up and each take a couple home with us?"

They couldn't be on their own in their current state. It was too dangerous.

Sheriff Hugo groaned. "My place isn't really kid friendly."

"I'll take Maeve and Juliet," Astrid offered.

Well, that was a no-brainer.

"I suppose I'm best suited to take Lady Weatherby," Professor Holmes said. "I can take Stan as well."

Lucy chewed her lip. "I'll see if Elsa can come to the Mayor's Mansion and take care of her mother."

"That still leaves Lord Gilder, Wayne, and Lorenzo," I said. If Gareth could interact with others, I'd consider taking Lord Gilder, but I didn't feel comfortable having the head of the vampires alone in the house with me.

"I'll send my owl with a note to the pack about Lorenzo," Professor Holmes said. "They'll want to deal with him, I imagine."

Sheriff Hugo groaned. "Fine. I'll take Wayne and Lord Gilder. They're both familiar with my place anyway."

I waited until arrangements were made and most of the afflicted were out of the Great Hall before focusing on the investigation. Professor Holmes summoned Ginger to take Lady Weatherby and Stan to his house and watch them until he came home. Members of the mayor's security team escorted her back to the mansion where Elsa awaited her.

Only Professor Holmes, Lucy, and I remained.

"We need to figure out who had an issue with the council," I said.

"I can think of someone right off the tip of my wings," Lucy said. "I was getting my hair done in Glow and overheard Marissa complaining about Maeve McCullen just yesterday."

"Who's Marissa?" I asked.

"A siren who performs at the playhouse with Maeve. She was upset about not getting a part she wanted."

"Well, that's a good start," I said. "Where's the best place to find Marissa?"

Lucy chewed her lip thoughtfully. "I know she goes to knitting class for stress relief. That might be the best time to corner her."

"Great, thanks. I'll check it out."

Professor Holmes chimed in. "If Marissa isn't our spell caster, it's possible that someone is overreacting to a decision the council made."

That made sense. The council made a lot of unpopular decisions. Residents constantly complained about the various rules and regulations that kept Spellbound in check.

"How do we figure out the recent issues they've decided?" I asked.

"That's easy," Lucy said. "The Book of Minutes and Minutiae will tell us."

I blinked. "The what?"

"The minutes from the council meetings," she replied. "Mayor Knightsbridge usually keeps the book in her office, but it would be here now, since they were at a meeting."

Right.

She flew up to the dais and retrieved the book. "What's the point of having the mayor's assistant as a friend if I can't come through in a crisis?"

"Lucy, this is brilliant," I said, turning to the most recent entry. "Thank you so much."

"It's supposed to be super duper confidential," Lucy said, frowning. "Please don't tell anyone you read it."

"Don't worry," I reassured her. "The way the gossip mill works in this town, everyone will assume I heard the information from someone else."

"Too true," Professor Holmes chimed in. "Now let's see if the minutes from the last couple of meetings tell us anything."

"This one has potential," I said, tapping the page. "An artist was denied permission to do a public show." I squinted, trying to read the rest. "Looks like he wanted to paint in the town square or something but the council said no."

"Oh." Lucy's eyes lit up. "Is that Lachlan?"

"That's what it looks like," I said. "Do you know him?" The name sounded familiar.

"A little bit," Lucy said. "He's been to the Mayor's Mansion for events. He's quite a character."

I snapped my fingers. "I remember where I saw his name. It was a sign at the Spellbound Care Home, the last time Daniel and I were there to volunteer."

"He's hosting an art class?" Professor Holmes asked.

"Something like that," I said. "I didn't really pay attention, but I'll find out. It might be a good opportunity to question him without raising suspicion."

"Imagine how excited all of the care home residents will be if they find out Lachlan can turn them into children again," Lucy said.

"They're still in their adult bodies," I reminded her. "I picture many broken hips and a few other orthopedic injuries."

Professor Holmes wore his approving Gandalf expression. Or was it Dumbledore? I couldn't decide.

"Sometimes you are wise beyond your years, Emma," he said.

"Thanks, Gan…I mean, Professor."

"Who else looks worth a visit?" Lucy asked, returning my attention to the book.

We read through the minutes of one last meeting before completing the priority list. The artist, an herbologist, and…

"Octavia Minor?" Professor Holmes queried, glancing at my notes. "Are you certain that's wise?" Octavia Minor was my neighbor and the grand matriarch of the harpies. A woman not to be trifled with, lest you end up in her trifle.

"She lodged a complaint with the council and they rebuffed her," I said. "She's a vindictive old woman. How can she not be included?"

"Because she might eat us," Lucy replied.

I sighed. "She lives next door. In my experience, neighbors don't eat neighbors."

"In your experience, people don't have horns and wings either," Lucy pointed out.

Fair enough.

"I'll stop by when I get a chance. I promise to keep it casual," I said. "They like to serve tea and finger sandwiches."

"Word of advice," Lucy said. "Make sure they aren't made out of actual fingers."

"And bring Sedgwick," Professor Holmes advised.

"He's not an attack dog." I said. "He's a cantankerous owl."

"No matter," Professor Holmes said. "He has sharp claws and an attitude."

"But I have a wand," I said.

Professor Holmes eyed me skeptically. "Yes, I've been at the receiving end of some of your… efforts. Be careful with it, Emma. The last thing you want to do is aggravate a harpy, least of all Octavia."

I shuddered. If I managed to aggravate Octavia Minor, I had no doubt that it would, indeed, be the last thing I ever did.

CHAPTER 4

❦

"You look worn out," Althea said, when I entered my office. "Are you not sleeping again?"

"Sleep is fine," I replied. "Just new stress that I wasn't anticipating." I told her about the current state of the town council.

"That can't be good," Althea said. "I remember some of those members when they actually *were* children." She whistled. "Train wreck city."

"I just wanted to grab a few books from here and start investigating."

"Sorry. Duty first." Althea handed me a file. "Some light reading before your appointment today."

"Would it kill you to give me a file the day before a client is due to arrive?"

Her snakes hissed loudly, sensing her irritation. "Gareth never complained about my timing."

Her assertion was easy enough to check and she knew it, so I had to assume it was true. Nevertheless, it would be easier for me to speak with my client if I had a little more lead time.

I opened the file and reviewed the summary. A werewolf accused of aggravated assault. "This happened at the Horned Owl?"

"That's what it says," Althea said. "I don't spend any time there myself, so I wouldn't know."

I spent plenty of time at the Horned Owl, but I hadn't heard about this incident. My eyes widened when I saw the name of the victim. Edgar.

"Edgar, the vampire?" I queried.

"Yes, he was a friend of Gareth's."

"I know. I met him on the golf course." When I first arrived in town, I went to see Gareth's friends at the Spellbound Country Club. That's when I met Demetrius Hunt, Samson, and Edgar.

I pondered the information in the file. "At least Edgar is a vampire. He would have needed to do a lot worse than a beer bottle to do any real damage."

"True. Still, I've heard that Russ has a bad temper. Maybe this is his comeuppance."

Everything I knew about Russ was contained in this file and that was exactly how I liked it. I didn't want my impression to be colored by other people's experiences with him.

"Thank you, Althea. How long do I have?"

"An hour. I'm running out to lunch. Can I get you anything?"

"No thanks. I want to power through this. I'll eat later."

She continued to stand there for a moment, staring at me. I glanced up from the file.

"Is everything okay?"

"It's not my place," she said, "but I feel like you haven't been eating that much lately. Are you handling everything…okay?"

Althea was perceptive. Truth be told, my appetite had waned since I'd attended the Spellbound High School dance with Daniel, the fallen angel and my self-proclaimed spirit animal. I was trying very hard to ignore the fact that I was in love with him. It seemed my body was selling me out.

"I'm good. Thank you for asking."

"If you're interested, I can recommend someone for you to talk to. Let me know."

I inclined my head. "You mean like a therapist?"

"Exactly. I'd encouraged Gareth to go at one point when he and Alison were having issues, but he refused. He was stubborn like that. I'd really appreciate it if you were less stubborn." She gave me a pointed look.

A therapist. I'd never been to one, despite being a prime candidate in the human world. My grandparents didn't believe in therapy. They'd decided that true grit was all I needed to cope with the death of my parents. I wasn't completely messed up, so maybe they were onto something.

"I'll take it under advisement, Althea. I'd better get started on this file," I said.

The Gorgon took the hint and returned to her office.

I was still reading an hour later when my client arrived. Russ looked like many of the other werewolves I'd met in town. Thick, dark hair. A muscular body. A swagger. The package screamed werewolf with an attitude.

"You must be Russ," I said.

He dropped into the chair in front of me and put his feet up on the edge of my desk. "So you're the infamous Emma. Alex told me about you. I think we're going to have a lot of fun together."

I gave his feet a gentle push off the desk. "Fun is not how I would describe this. You're charged with aggravated assault. That's very serious."

He chewed on his fingernails. Another werewolf trait I'd noticed. "The dude is a vampire. If I'd had deadly intent, then

I would've used a stake, am I right?" For a split second, I thought he'd try to high-five me.

"So tell me what happened. You were drinking in the bar and something made you angry. Why did you throw the bottle at Edgar?"

"I went there with a few of my buddies after work to blow off steam. Edgar was there with a group of friends from the country club. I wasn't trying to hit Edgar. It was an accident."

"Were you drunk?"

"I'd say so. I'd had several beers at that point, plus three shots of Bitter Apple."

I needed to look into werewolf metabolism. It sounded like a lot, but with paranormal creatures, you could never be too sure.

"You said it was an accident. You didn't mean to hit Edgar. If you didn't mean to hit him, why did you throw the bottle?"

Russ turned his gaze to the floor. "I didn't throw the bottle at Edgar. I threw it at Henrik."

"The berserker barista from Brew-Ha-Ha?"

"That's the guy. Every time I go in there, he doesn't give me the heart in the foam on my latte. It pissed me off. When I saw him in the pub, I lost it."

He threw a bottle at the berserker's head because he wasn't getting foam hearts on his lattes? Althea was right. This guy had a major issue with his temper.

"With all due respect, don't you think your response was disproportionate to the event?"

Russ looked at me blankly. "Could you maybe use smaller words?"

I inhaled sharply. "Why do you think Henrik doesn't give you foam hearts? You're obviously taking it very personally."

"I used to date his younger sister, Gigi," he said. "She

broke up with me about a month ago. I feel like he's deliberately not giving me the hearts to taunt me."

"Why did you and Gigi break up?"

He continued to gnaw on his nails. "She felt like we were getting too serious. She wanted to take a break, but we all know what that really means."

"Was Gigi in the bar that night?" I asked.

His brow lifted. "She was. How did you know?"

"I didn't know. I just wondered whether that was what set you off. You'd had a lot to drink. I thought maybe something prompted it. Gigi was the most obvious trigger."

He nodded. "Yeah, she was there with her brother. When she saw me with my friends, she left." His expression clouded over. "She didn't have to leave because of me. I wouldn't have bothered her. She said she wanted space and I had every intention of giving it to her." He gave me a sincere look. "If you love something, you set it free, right?"

My thoughts inevitably turned to Daniel. "Yes, Russ. You do. And if you're freakishly lucky, it comes back to you in the end."

"I'm sorry about Edgar," he said. "I've got no beef with him. Of course, now it's drummed up all sorts of problems between the werewolves and the vampires."

Oh. That didn't sound good.

"What type of problems? Do Lorenzo and Lord Gilder know?"

"Not sure. If it gets out of control, though, they'll know soon enough."

"How is Edgar? Have you checked on him?"

"Of course I did," he said vehemently. "I'm not an animal."

That was debatable. "Is he still at the healers' office or is he home?"

"He's home," Russ said. "He's confined to his coffin for now. He said he'll be up and around soon enough."

Russ must've done some serious damage with a broken bottle to knock a vampire out of commission like that. Werewolf strength in action.

"I heard you're trying to do something about lesser sentences for criminals," Russ said. "When I first heard about it, I wasn't so sure. But now that I'm facing charges, I have a different attitude." He smiled vaguely. "So have you made any progress with that?"

"As a matter of fact, I'm planning to attend the next council meeting to raise the issue. It's tomorrow."

He brightened. "So is there a chance that if I'm convicted, my sentence will be reduced?"

"I doubt it, Russ. Work like that can take years. It won't happen overnight." Nothing good ever did.

Russ slumped in the chair. "It was stupid of me to throw that bottle. I should've hit my mark. I have a great arm. I never should've missed."

"Russ, you do realize you'd still be sitting here if you'd managed to hit Henrik instead of Edgar?" Not to mention that Henrik could have been killed. Berserkers weren't immortal like vampires. In reality, Russ was lucky that he hit Edgar instead.

"Oh, I know," he said, with a regretful sigh. "But at least I would've felt better about it."

When I left the office, I noticed the town council and Stan in a nearby park. Lucy was attempting to keep them occupied with various bits of playground equipment. Maeve and Juliet were content on the swings, singing a nursery rhyme I didn't recognize.

"Help," Lucy said, gripping my arm upon arrival. "I'm running out of ideas. Lorenzo keeps barking at everyone and laughing and Lord Gilder tried to bite the mayor when she sat at the top of the slide and refused to go down."

I noticed Chairman Meow in a patch of grass, batting at a dandelion. Lady Weatherby was stretched out on her stomach beside him, staring intently at a single blade of grass.

"Lady Weatherby's familiar is here," I said.

"I know," Lucy said, with an exaggerated sigh. "She refused to leave him home. I'm pretty sure he's reverted to the behavior of a kitten. When I picked them up, I saw him scratching the back of Lady Weatherby's velvet sofa."

"He wasn't in the Great Hall when the spell was cast," I said.

"No, but he's her familiar," Lucy explained. "It must be the psychic link."

I glanced around the playground. "Where's everyone else? I thought Professor Holmes was helping you."

"Boyd needed him. A spell to fix the roof of the healer's office or something. He'll be back soon."

Based on the rowdy behavior in front of me, it wouldn't be soon enough. I dropped to my knees beside Lady Weatherby to see what she was doing.

"Are you trying to do a spell?" I asked.

She continued to fixate on the blade of grass. "No," she replied. "I just can't believe how green this grass is. Have you ever seen such a brilliant color? It's magical all by itself."

Her childlike wonder was surprisingly sweet. "There's magic all around us," I said. "It doesn't always need to come from a wand."

"Or a witch," she agreed. "Maeve's singing voice is magical and she's not enchanted."

I paused for a moment to listen. "It really is."

Lord Gilder and Lorenzo landed on the grass beside us

with a thud. Each was trying to sink his teeth into the flesh of the other one.

"I'm stronger," Lorenzo growled.

They were in the bodies of an adult werewolf and an adult vampire. I had no way of breaking up this fight without risking my life.

I noticed the professor's broomstick leaning against the frame of the swing set and picked it up.

"Okay, I want everybody's attention." I tried to use my best authoritative voice. "Now."

"You're not my mother. You can't tell me what to do," Maeve said, folding her arms.

"I can and I will," I said. "I'm in charge until further notice."

"You can't be in charge," Wayne said. "You haven't lived here long enough. No one will listen to you."

The troll was sensible even under a youth spell.

"What's the broomstick for?" Lady Weatherby asked. "We all know you can't fly one." She giggled and I chucked the broomstick at her head.

She ducked and turned to glare at me. "Hey!"

That got Lord Gilder and Lorenzo's attention. They stopped fighting and gaped at me.

"If you can dodge a broomstick, then you can dodge a ball," I yelled. I was fairly confident they'd never seen the movie Dodgeball.

"What ball?" Juliet demanded.

I turned to Lucy. "Um, can you magic me up a small, red rubber ball?"

Using her wand, Lucy pointed at a round stone on the ground and muttered an enchantment. The stone expanded and morphed into a red rubber ball.

"And a whistle, too, while you're at it."

Lucy pointed her wand at a piece of mulch and abracadabra-ed it.

"Perfect," I said. I put the rope of the whistle around my neck and held up the ball. "Listen up. This is the ball you need to dodge. You'll be split into two teams, separated by a line in the dirt. The object is to hit the players on the opposite team with the ball without crossing the center line until you're the only team with members left."

Mayor Knightsbridge snatched the ball from my hands and immediately slammed it into the side of Lord Gilder's head. The vampire rubbed his temple and showed his fangs to the feisty fairy.

"Don't you threaten me with those toothpicks," Mayor Knightsbridge said. "I'll shove my wand right up your…"

I blew a whistle. "Okay, kids. I will divide the teams."

Once the game started, they seemed to settle down. The play was rough, as I expected given they were in their adult bodies.

By the time Professor Holmes returned, the game was half over. The defeated players sat cross-legged on the sidelines, cheering on their teammates.

"What's happening here?" he asked. "Why are you letting them attack each other?"

"It's dodgeball," I said. "They're playing the game."

"And very well, too," Lucy added. "They've been a delight to watch."

"What spell did you use to get them to behave?" Professor Holmes asked, incredulous.

"No spell," I said. "Just a few clear parameters and a central goal."

"Impressive," he said, just as Lorenzo attempted to turn furry in the middle of the game.

"No shifting, Mancini," I bellowed, blowing my whistle. "That's rule number fifteen, remember?"

The fur receded and Lorenzo put himself in timeout.

"I need someone else to take over when this game is finished," I said. "I have work to do."

"Yes, Ginger and Meg will be stepping in after their aerobics class," Professor Holmes said. "Have you had a chance to speak with anyone else on the list?"

"Not yet," I said. "I heard that some people thinks it's a coup attempt and Sheriff Hugo is questioning known subversives."

The professor's brow wrinkled. "Then wouldn't the new leaders have taken over by now?"

"Exactly." I tucked my wand in the back of my waistband. "He's wasting his time."

"More importantly, he's wasting valuable time," Lucy said. "We don't know what the repercussions are if we can't change them back quickly. What if they're stuck like this forever?"

I shuddered. It was one thing to be locked in a childlike state for a brief period, but to live out an extended or immortal life as a child trapped in an adult body…It was a far worse fate than simply being trapped in Spellbound. They were the governing arm of this town and their fates rested in our hands.

The ball froze in midair and the remaining players dove to the ground, expecting it to land nearby.

"Lady Weatherby, you're in violation of rule twelve," I said. "That's a timeout for you."

"It wasn't me," she protested. "You weren't even looking."

"I have eyes in the back of my head," I said. Totally believable in Spellbound.

The ball dropped onto the center line and Lord Gilder grabbed it.

"Make way for your lord and master," he cried, sending the ball careening into the mayor's stomach. She doubled over and let loose a string of swear words that burned everyone's ears.

"Inappropriate language and a direct hit. Mayor Knightsbridge, you're out," I said, blowing the whistle.

We had them under control right now, but for how long? I only hoped we could reverse the spell before it was too late.

CHAPTER 5

I FORCED myself to visit the Minor house and speak with Octavia before I lost my nerve. As though I'd flashed the bat signal, Sedgwick appeared overhead as I walked up the front path to the harpies' house.

"I probably could use a bat signal with you," I mused. "You'd think there were actual bats flying around up there and swoop right in."

What in Athena's name is a bat signal? he asked.

"Never mind," I said. "Will you perch on the widow's walk and wait for me in case things go south?"

You know I'm uncomfortable hanging around here, he said.

"And I'm uncomfortable sticking an apple in my mouth and climbing onto her dinner plate, but that's what I'm about to do because it's necessary."

The front door opened, causing me to squeal like a pig. The irony wasn't lost on me.

"This is an outrage," a voice said sharply and the hair on my arms stood on end.

The matriarch's regular voice was frightening enough. Her angry voice was enough to make giants quake.

Octavia stood in front of me in human form. My feet begged me to run, but I stood rooted to the ground. "Octavia, is everything okay?"

"If by okay, you mean that werewolf piss will make the herbs in my garden grow, then yes everything is stellar." She stepped onto the porch, hands on hips. She radiated anger and aggression, her usual qualities.

"Werewolf urine? What do you mean?"

"It seems that the shifters think it's a free-for-all now that the town council is more useless than normal."

Already? How did this sleepy town manage to move at breakneck speed? It was mind-boggling.

"They're ignoring the ordinances and doing whatever the hell they please. I even caught two werelions fornicating on the edge of my property in their animal forms." She bristled. "It sounded like the murder of a small village."

I couldn't decide which incident bothered her more—the fact that her garden smelled like werewolf pee or the fact that someone else was getting busy other than her. The harpy looked old enough to have dated the Crypt Keeper. I wasn't sure how busy she was capable of getting under any circumstances.

"You can file a complaint with the sheriff's office," I said.

"The sheriff's office," she repeated with a scowl. "The first order of business when the council is back in their right mind is to replace that good-for-nothing centaur. This is his big chance to prove himself and he's blowing it majorly."

I was inclined to agree. If ever there was a time to step up and prove his mettle, this was it. Unfortunately, his bad habits were so ingrained that he seemed incapable of performing his duties.

"You should speak to Astrid," I said. "She's highly competent."

Octavia grunted as her gaze moved across her front

garden. "Have you had any issues with shifters on your property?"

"I don't think so." I was pretty sure I'd notice noise that sounded like the murder of a small village. I wasn't exactly a sound sleeper.

She narrowed her eyes at me and a shiver ran down my spine. "Why do you think that is?"

I honestly had no idea. My yard was as close to the woods as hers with the added bonus that my house wasn't full of vindictive harpies.

"Your guess is as good as mine," I said.

She inclined her head in a birdlike fashion. "Did you have the coven ward your property?"

"No, although it has come up in conversation on occasion." I certainly wasn't capable of doing it myself. I lacked the level of skill required.

"Well, I hope the spell gets reversed soon before this town plunges into chaos. There are far too many dangerous creatures here to allow entropy to set in. If we're not careful, we'll have the inmates taking over the prison."

"I couldn't agree more."

"I need to head over to the Wish Market. My daughters claim to be too busy to pick up a few necessities for the woman who suffered through birth for them. Don't take it personally, but I have more important things to do than blow oxygen in your direction."

"Um, technically we breathe out carbon dioxide."

"You're a real oddball. You know that?"

Octavia ambled down the porch steps and reverted to her harpy form. I watched in awe as the aging human woman shifted into the form of a part bird, part woman. Wings sprouted on her back and sharp talons cracked through her knuckles. To my relief, she didn't turn back to look at me before taking to the air. I knew it was a face that would give me nightmares. With a loud shriek, she disappeared over the treetops.

Once my heart rate slowed, I headed home. If nothing else, I knew with certainty that Octavia played no role in the youth spell. She relied on the town rules and regulations to get her way and was unhappy with the present situation. She was the last person to want the council incapacitated.

I sighed. One suspect down. About a hundred to go.

Despite the town council youth crisis, I had to keep my eye on my own client's ball. I decided to visit Edgar to check on his progress and follow up on Russ's case. As a close friend of Gareth's, I knew Edgar would talk to me.

His house was located on the north side of town, not too far from the country club. Even though it had a wraparound front porch and a colorful exterior, the style was more Southern Gothic than Victorian. There were even paddle fans installed on the porch ceiling and I wondered what powered them. Presumably magical energy.

I debated whether I should knock first and go inside. If Edgar was stuck in his coffin, then he wouldn't be able to come to the door. Before I could decide, the front door opened and I was greeted by a bald, stocky man with stooped shoulders.

"Yes?" he said.

"Hello," I said, trying to hide my surprise. I didn't expect Edgar to have a butler. "I came by to see Edgar. I heard about his accident and would like to see how he's doing."

The butler squinted at me. "'Twas no accident, miss. Chucked the bottle straight at his head, he did." He pulled open the door and stepped aside. "Your name, miss?"

"Emma Hart," I said, and stepped into the grand foyer. It was nothing like Gareth's house. When I'd first arrived, the walls were dark and dismal and the blackout shades made the interior feel too much like a haunted house. Edgar's house, on the other hand, would have fit neatly in the pages of Architectural Digest. Everything was tastefully done, from the intricately carved banister to the gleaming hardwood floors. I had to hand it to these vampires. If it had been me, I would have built my house out of bricks and made all of the flooring out of tile. To their credit, they seemed very comfortable being surrounded by potential stakes.

I followed the Hunchback of Jeeves down a back staircase. Like Gareth, Edgar seems to prefer the lower level for his master suite. It was only when I heard voices that I realized Edgar already had company.

"Master Edgar, a visitor. May I present Miss Emma Hart?"

He stepped aside and I saw the group of vampires gathered around Edgar's coffin, laughing and drinking. Demetrius was there, looking amazing as always in a snug T-shirt and formfitting pants. His dark eyes lit up when he saw me.

"Emma," he said, coming over to greet me. "I wasn't expecting to see you here."

"I heard about Edgar and I wanted to see if he was okay," I said. "Gareth would never forgive me if I didn't check on him."

At the mention of Gareth's name, everyone stopped talking. It suddenly occurred to me that I'd never told them about my ability to see Gareth in the here and now. I sucked in a breath. Now was as good a time as any.

"Gareth sends his regards. He would have loved to come himself, but he's restricted in his movements. We're working on it, though."

They all stared at me, silent and deadly serious.

A vampire I didn't recognize sipped from his blood red cocktail and said, "Then the Lord said to Samuel, 'Behold, I am about to do a thing in Israel at which the two ears of everyone who hears it will tingle.'"

Edgar rolled his eyes. "Dante, how many times have I told you not to quote Scripture in my house?"

"You can tell me as often as you like, but you can't stop the word of God," Dante replied. "Nothing can."

I thought it was best to stay out of their disagreement. The only thing worse than a religious disagreement was a religious disagreement between vampires.

"You can communicate with our Gareth?" Samson asked. For a group of undead, they seemed remarkably startled over someone communicating with the dead.

"Yes," I admitted. "I've been able to see and hear him for some time now. I wasn't sure whether I should keep it secret, so I didn't exactly shout it from the hilltops. A lot of people seem to know, though, so I think it's time to come clean."

"Does the coven know?" Edgar asked.

"They do. They weren't sure what to make of it at first."

Dante studied me closely. "And do they know now?"

"Not yet," I said. "But I think it's good for Gareth to still feel a part of the community. If everyone knows he's around, that might lift his spirits." Or was it spirit?

"I'd love to see him when I'm feeling better," Edgar said. "Perhaps we could try a séance." The other vampires murmured in agreement.

"A séance?" I asked. "Is that really something that would work? When I asked..." I nearly said Raisa, but I quickly realized that was a situation I needed to keep to myself for now. I got the distinct impression that Lady Weatherby and Professor Holmes wanted to keep my interaction with the dead witch under wraps. "I was under the impression that there were very few seers in town."

"Kassandra," Dante said. "She'd be perfect."

"You just want to ogle her neck during the séance," Demetrius accused.

"And you don't?" Dante challenged him. "He that is without sin among you, let him first cast a stone at her."

Edgar rolled his eyes again. "Last warning, Dante. Don't make me throw you out of my house."

"Would you be amenable to hosting the séance at your house?" Samson asked.

"Would you mind if I checked with Gareth first?" I asked. "I'm sure it will be fine, but I wouldn't feel right agreeing to it without his permission."

"Understandable," Edgar said. "You are such a reasonable girl. A fine choice for his replacement."

Finally. Perfect opening. "On that note," I said, "would you mind giving me your version of events from the night at the Horned Owl?"

Edgar's expression softened. "Right. I see. You're representing Russ, are you not?"

I shrugged. "The public defender's job never ends."

"We were all there," Demetrius said. "We saw Russ throw the bottle and hit Edgar."

"Russ doesn't dispute that he threw the bottle," I said, "but he says his target was Henrik."

"Henrik was in the next group over," Samson said. "The bottle looped left before it reached the berserkers."

"Is there any reason you can think of that Russ would lie about his intended victim?" I asked. "If he meant to hit Edgar, why not just say so?"

"To my knowledge, I have no quarrel with the werewolf," Edgar said.

"Other than the fact that you dislike shifters," Dante added.

Edgar glared at his friend. "I'm not a racist. I simply prefer my own kind, a sentiment I tend to keep to myself.

Russ had no reason to attack me."

"So did you assume it was an accident from the beginning?" I asked.

"I don't suppose I gave it much thought," Edgar said. "I simply believed he enjoyed one too many shots of whatever toxins he was injecting himself with that night and threw the bottle in a typical aggressive werewolf fashion."

"Was there anyone at the pub that night with a reason to attack you?" I asked.

Samson snapped his fingers. "Now that you mention it, I do remember seeing Brion there."

Edgar groaned. "Do you have to mention him? My drink has soured."

"It's a Bloody Mary," Samson said. "It's already sour."

"Who's Brion?" I asked.

"A genie from the country club," Edgar said, with a dismissive wave.

"Edgar had his privileges revoked for cheating," Demetrius said. "Brion's no longer a member of the club."

"How did he cheat?" I asked. I didn't know enough about golf to understand what would constitute cheating.

"He used his magic on the golf course," Edgar said. "That's strictly prohibited for obvious reasons."

"And you saw him?" I asked.

"Several times," Edgar admitted. "I let it go at first because he wasn't a party to our game, but it began to interfere with my own enjoyment."

"Magic makes things too easy," Demetrius said. "The rules are in place to make sure everyone is on even ground. It's more fun that way."

For a vampire with a bad boy reputation, Demetrius seemed surprisingly reasonable and law abiding. Maybe his penchant for bad boy behavior was only tied to his libido.

"I guess it's worth a conversation with Brion," I said. "See if he holds a grudge."

"Speaking of grudges," Samson said, "I hear that Lord Gilder lost at dodgeball. Was he unhappy?"

"You could say that," I said. "At the end of the game, he bit the ball with his fangs and deflated it."

The other vampires laughed.

"I've often wondered what he was like as a child," Edgar said. "I hate to be missing it."

"We're looking for a constant rotation of babysitters," I said. "But I think you need to be in good condition to look after him. He's…temperamental." It occurred to me that I should really get moving.

"Feel free to send him my way," Demetrius offered. "I wouldn't mind the opportunity to put Lord Gilder in his place. The devil knows I'll never get the chance again."

"Thanks, Dem," I said. "I may take you up on your offer."

He inched closer and gazed at me with those dark, tempting eyes. "While we're on the subject, are there any other offers of mine you're willing to take me up on?"

I groped for words. His sex appeal was just so…appealing. "Not today," I squeaked. "But thanks."

CHAPTER 6

I PLACED a headband on my head and Sedgwick nearly fell off his perch.

What do you think you're wearing? he asked.

"What does it look like?" I asked, turning to face him.

He squawked and flew back to the window. *You have whiskers!*

"Today is the cat party for Magpie," I said. "So I'm dressed as a cat. I made headbands and whiskers for all the girls." I touched the triangle ears on top of the headband.

You look ridiculous, he scoffed. *If you're planning to crawl around on all fours and lick those hairy arms of yours, I'm not sticking around to watch.*

"I don't have hairy arms," I objected, but he was already gone.

Now that my transformation was complete, I retrieved a comb from my dresser and went downstairs to find Magpie. I found him on the windowsill, basking in the sunlight. For some reason, that struck me as funny. Although I knew typical cats liked to warm their bodies in the sun, I didn't think Magpie qualified. I associated him with darkness, probably because his owner was a vampire. Or because he sucked the souls of the innocent while they slept. Either one.

"Listen up, Magpie," I said, creeping toward the windowsill. "The other cats will be here soon. They're coming here for your benefit and you need to be a good host." I held my breath and reached for him, wielding the comb like a sword.

"What in the devil are you trying to do to my cat?" Gareth demanded.

Magpie hissed and dodged my grasp, leaping to the floor.

"I want to comb the millimeter of hair that he has," I said. "He needs to make an effort."

"In case you haven't noticed, Magpie does a wonderful job of grooming himself."

I glanced down at the black and white beast with his half-chewed ear and angry face. "He looks like he lost a street fight with a pack of werehyenas and had to dig himself out of a back alley dumpster."

Gareth gasped. "Bite your tongue, Emma Hart. That's the meanest thing I've ever heard you say."

The wind chimes sounded and I tucked the comb into my back pocket. "They're here. Be on your best behavior, please."

I opened the door to a small parade of witches and their cat familiars. "Come on in. Welcome to the 'pawty.'"

"Emma, you look so cute," Begonia said, stroking my whiskers.

"Oh, thanks for reminding me." I retrieved the bag of headbands and whiskers from the banister. "One for each of you."

The girls put on their cat essentials without complaint. Magpie lurked in the living room doorway, assessing the situation. His tail flicked left and right. I had the feeling that he and I were going to differ on what constituted 'best behavior.'

Because they were familiars, the cats' personalities tended to reflect their witch partners'. Begonia's cat was upbeat and pleasant. Laurel's cat was inquisitive. Sophie's cat was sweet and trusting, while Millie's cat was intelligent with an air of haughtiness.

As the four cats moved toward the living room, Magpie made his displeasure known. The hissing was more powerful than seemed possible from a single cat. It sounded like a thousand worker bees alerting the hive to danger.

"What's wrong with him?" I asked.

"Nothing's wrong with him," Gareth said. "He's being a cat. This is his territory and it's being invaded by walking balls of fluff."

"They're not walking balls of fluff," I said. "They have just the right amount of hair for cats."

Begonia bent over to stroke Kitty. "How dare you. She is not a fluff ball. Show some respect."

"Magpie, don't be rude," I scolded him. "You're the host. You set the tone."

He swished his tail angrily and stalked toward the kitchen.

"Give him time," Gareth encouraged. "He's used to spending time alone. He's an introvert."

The witches followed me into the living room where I had the table ready for our guests.

Millie stopped and stared at the place settings. "Great sun and moon, what is this for?" She picked up one of the conical hats.

"It's a party," I said. "I bought party hats."

"But we already have headbands." Millie held it up to her head. "How do you expect these to fit us? They're made for…"

"Cats," I finished for her. "They're not for us." If Chairman

Meow could wear a headdress with tiny antlers, I figured these cats could wear jovial party hats.

Sophie burst into laughter. "You expect our cats to wear party hats? Do you know anything about cats?"

My cheeks warmed. "They hiss a lot, like tuna, and fill up a litter box more than seems physically possible."

Millie set the hat back on the table. "And they don't do party hats. At least Poca won't. I can't speak for the others."

"I think they're adorable," Begonia said, and held one out to her familiar. "What do you think, Kitty? Any interest?"

The tiger cat sniffed the hat and mewled before backing away.

"She says it's a nice thought," Begonia said diplomatically.

"I have more than party hats," I said, rushing to the other end of the table. "Look, I bought tuna cookies."

"Oh, they're in the shape of a fish," Sophie said. "How cute." Momo jumped onto the table and batted the cookie with her paw.

"She can have it if she wants," I said. "We don't stand on ceremony here, do we Magpie?"

The hairless wonder had wandered in behind everyone to investigate. He leaped onto the table, scattering two party hats and knocking a tuna cookie onto the floor. Delilah dove for it and carried the cookie away in her mouth before another cat could swipe it.

"There's enough for everyone," I said. "Magpie, why don't you try one?"

"He's not comfortable with crowds," Gareth said, framed in the doorway.

"These are all perfectly nice cats," I said. "And he's used to my friends by now."

"Doesn't mean he likes it," Gareth replied.

"Why don't we leave them alone for a few minutes?" I

suggested, ushering my friends out of the living room and into the kitchen.

Laurel lingered behind, glancing over her shoulder.

"Laurel, what's wrong?" I asked.

"What if he attacks them?" she asked, uncertain. "Delilah isn't a fighter. She won't know how to defend herself."

"She has claws, right?" I asked.

"Don't be a helicopter witch," Millie snapped. "Delilah needs to learn how to socialize with other cats without you monitoring her every move. You baby her too much."

"Because she's a baby," Laurel shot back.

"I don't think Delilah has a problem socializing," Begonia said. "I think Laurel is just concerned about her interactions with Magpie. He's not a familiar. He won't have the same…" She groped for the right words.

"They're acting like Magpie is some kind of common street thug," Gareth complained, following us into the kitchen. "I'm not a witch, but he's my familiar, or as close to one as a vampire can get."

My heart softened. "Relax," I said. "It's going to be fine. Magpie just needs to get used to having other cats in the house. As long as he knows they're not moving in and using his litter box, I think he'll come around."

"You stay here," Gareth said. "I'll keep an eye on things in there."

"Gareth is going to supervise," I told them. "If he so much as swipes in a familiar's direction, he'll report back."

We gathered around the kitchen counter and I could see the tension in Laurel's shoulders. I tried to distract her with conversation about the town council.

"I spoke with Octavia Minor," I said, "but I don't think she had a hand in the youth spell."

"Of course not," Millie scoffed. "If she did, she wouldn't waste it on the town council. She'd use it on herself."

Fair point.

"Is it wrong that I enjoy seeing Lady Weatherby singing to herself and making daisy chains?" Sophie asked.

"I helped her make some yesterday," Laurel said proudly. "We had a great time together. I showed her the spell to change the color of a ladybug and she acted like it was the most amazing thing she'd ever seen."

"She taught us that spell." Begonia began to laugh, but a loud screech interrupted her.

Uh oh.

We raced to the living room to see that the party had gone horribly awry. A trail of broken fish cookies ran along the edge of the table and spilled onto the floor. Pieces of the shredded party hats were scattered around the room. Why had Gareth not alerted us?

Millie sniffed the air. "Do I smell cat pee?"

Begonia covered her nose and mouth. "Very potent cat pee. What does he drink—acid?"

"Don't get involved," Gareth warned, observing from the sidelines. "Let them sort it out."

I watched as Magpie pinned Momo to the table and hissed in her face. Then, to my amazement, he gingerly lifted his paw and Momo escaped to the floor, curling around Sophie's feet.

"She's scared out of her mind," Sophie said, scooping up her cat and clutching her to her chest.

Magpie stood in the middle of the table and surveyed the carnage around him. He was like the T-Rex at the end of Jurassic Park, asserting his dominance over the other dinosaurs.

"It'll be fine now," Gareth assured us. "He's made his point."

His point? Sure enough, I watched as Magpie jumped down from the table and slowly approached Kitty.

"Is he stalking her?" I asked quietly.

Magpie's paw jutted out and tapped Kitty's tail. Kitty turned around and I was sure she would hiss. Instead, she began to chase him. Magpie zipped beneath the table with Kitty hot on his heels.

"Spell's bells," Begonia breathed. "They're playing."

One by one, the other cats joined in until they were all embroiled in some feline version of tag.

"This is great," I said. I'd never seen Magpie so playful. It gave me hope for our relationship.

"He just needed to set the rules," Gareth explained. "It's only when he feels safe that he feels free to let his guard down."

"Is that your special theory on cats?" I asked.

Gareth gave me a slight smile. "No, lass. That's my theory on everybody."

I pulled Sigmund into a parking lot in town, where I noticed an elf and a dwarf arguing by the entrance. I stopped and tapped the glass of my window, making it disappear.

"Is there a problem?" I asked.

The dwarf was red-faced and looked ready to erupt. "Sonny thinks he doesn't have to pay to park today."

I double-checked the sign. "It isn't past six o'clock. Why would you not have to pay, Sonny?"

The elf glared at me. "Why should anyone pay anything while the council is dismantled?"

"The council isn't dismantled," I argued. "They're on a temporary hiatus."

"While they're on hiatus, so am I," Sonny said. He stomped out of the parking lot without a backward glance.

"Can you call someone to give him a ticket?" I asked.

The dwarf blew out a breath. "This has been happening

all day. No one seems to think the rules apply while the council is out of commission."

This was an alarming development and seemed to fit with Octavia's experience. The last thing a town full of paranormals needed was a complete disregard for rules and regulations. As much as I mocked Spellbound's penchant for red tape, it served a purpose.

"You should let Sheriff Hugo and Deputy Astrid know," I said.

"I already did," he said. "They're too busy trying to keep the peace. Problems have been cropping up all over town."

Yikes. And here I was arriving for a knitting class. To be fair, I was investigating the spell on the council.

I pulled two coins from my handbag and gave them to the dwarf. "I'll pay for Sonny, too."

The redness faded from his plump face. "Thanks. There's an available spot straight down and to the left."

I parked the car and hurried to class. I didn't want to be late, especially when I'd never attended before.

The building was tucked on a side street behind Serendipity, one of the nicest restaurants in town. Once inside, a sign instructed me to head downstairs.

"Are you here to knit?" a friendly voice asked. A gnome. She was shorter than Myra, the church administrator, but with a more pleasant countenance.

"I'd like to learn," I lied. In truth, I would rather stick a knitting needle in my eye, but I had to take one for the team.

"We always welcome new students," the gnome said. "There are a few empty seats."

I quickly scanned the room for Marissa. With her flowing hair and flawless features, she was easy to spot. I noticed the empty chair beside her and made a beeline for it before anyone else could claim it.

"Oh, hello. I recognize you," someone said. "You're friends with my sister."

I turned to the young woman next to me. Tall, blond, and intimidating. "I didn't realize Astrid had a sister."

Her expression crumpled. "I'm Britta. Astrid's the successful one in the family. I'm her loser older sister."

"Britta, I'm sure that's not true," I said. "It's only that we tend to talk about work when we're together."

"Even at poker night?"

Oops. "You're more than welcome to join us for the next one." Whenever that was. I barely had time to keep up with what I *had* to do—forget about what I *wanted* to do.

The Valkyrie brightened. "I'd like that. I swear I won't lose my temper."

I gulped. Britta was a hothead? "Um, that would be appreciated."

"That's why she knits," the voice on the other side of me interjected. Marissa. "It calms her."

Britta smiled. "It's been a game changer."

I turned to the siren. "Hi, I'm Emma."

"Marissa. Nice to meet you."

The gnome dropped a woven basket next to my chair. It was filled with different colored balls of yarn and a set of knitting needles. "You'll be needing these."

"Thank you." I glanced around to see what projects others were working on. A sweater, a scarf, a hat, a blanket. I could knit absolutely none of those items. The best I could offer was to order Chinese food and use the knitting needles in lieu of chopsticks.

"How hard is it to knit a sock?" I asked.

Britta laughed. "One sock? Why bother?"

I shrugged. "Sentimental reasons. Socks used to have a way of disappearing on me." There'd been a dryer in the basement of my apartment building in Lemon Grove that was notorious for eating the mates to my socks. Thankfully, missing socks were no longer an issue for me in Spellbound. Talk about a game changer.

"I can help you with a sock," Marissa offered.

I kept my eyes on the ball of yarn in my lap, careful to seem nonchalant. "Someone mentioned that you're an actress," I said. "That must be exciting."

Marissa smiled brightly. "I am definitely living the dream. I know a lot of people complain about being trapped here, but I would never live anywhere else. I love the playhouse and I adore working with Maeve."

"Really?" I said. "I heard the two of you had a falling out recently."

She frowned. "I wouldn't call it a falling out. We had an argument, as creatives tend to do. We are very passionate about our art."

"What was the argument about?"

"I was supposed to play the role of Valerie in her new play, but, at the last minute, she decided that she wanted to play Valerie so she gave me the role of Moira instead."

"I take it Valerie is the lead role and Moira is a supporting role," I said.

"She's been promising me a lead role forever," she said. "I'm not getting any younger. I'm tired of waiting. She just can't seem to give up the limelight. And, of course, it's her playhouse. She can do whatever she likes."

"Well, it sounds like you tried to speak with her about it. What happened?"

I felt her anger simmering beneath the surface. She began to attack the ball of yarn with her knitting needles.

"She said I still wasn't ready. That Valerie was too complex of a character for me. Can you believe it? I mean, I know I'm not a banshee, but I understand death and depression. I'm a freakin' siren, for Poseidon's sake."

Since I knew that sirens were responsible for luring men to a watery grave, I didn't disagree with her.

"You must've been pretty angry," I said. "How did you handle it?"

She jabbed a knitting needle into the yarn. "I put glue on the handle of her brush in her dressing room."

An interesting choice for revenge. "So did her hand get stuck?"

Marissa pouted. "No, because the spell took hold of her before she showed up in her dressing room for rehearsal. She hasn't touched her brush for days. The glue is probably too hard now."

"But with Maeve in youth mode, doesn't that leave the role of Valerie to you?"

Marissa lit up like a Christmas tree. "Oh my gosh. I hadn't thought of that. You're totally right. I can play Valerie now. Rehearsals have been put on hold, but I think I'll summon everyone to the playhouse." She reached over and hugged me. "Emma, you are a genius."

Not really, since I'd believed Marissa was responsible. Now I was pretty confident the siren was not our culprit.

"Are you sure you're making a sock?" she asked, eyeing the monstrosity in my lap.

"I was thinking of making a sweater for my cat instead."

She looked unconvinced. "Why does your cat need a sweater? Doesn't it have a fur coat?"

"You would think," I said. "Magpie is a special case."

"Do you think he would wear a sweater? I imagine the cat might be resistant to clothing."

Magpie was resistant to everything. "It's the thought that counts." The thought that I might be able to use the sweater to smother Magpie the next time he tried to bite my ankle.

"I wish I was as good at witchcraft as you are at knitting," I said. It would save everyone around me a world of hurt.

"People like you and I are the lucky ones in this town," Marissa said. "You don't need to be good at magic when you have charm. People are just as likely to bend to your will when you show them kindness instead of a wand."

"I don't know about that," Britta said. "You can break every dish in someone's house and get them to bend to your will. It worked for me."

"Britta, remember why you're here," Marissa said.

Britta nodded, strips of blond hair falling in front of her face. "I'm channeling my rage into something productive."

Proudly, she held up her positive creation. With its obnoxious colors and confusing pattern, it was the angriest looking sweater I'd ever seen.

"That's wonderful," I choked out. "Who's it for?"

"Astrid. A peace offering."

"A peace…" I began. "Oh, the dishes you broke belong to her, I take it."

Britta nodded. "In my defense, they were butt ugly dishes."

I suddenly had second thoughts about inviting her to my house. I didn't want broken dishes or a sweater from Britta. In either case, Gareth might find a way to come back from the dead and kill her.

"So what do you think, Emma?" Marissa asked. "Is knitting for you?"

Now that I'd ruled out Marissa as a suspect, there was no need to struggle with the oversized chopsticks anymore.

I dropped the needles into my lap and sighed. "To be honest, knitting stresses me out."

Britta let out a loud whoop and broke a knitting needle over her thigh. "Thank the stars somebody said it. I don't like it either. Holding one of these suckers makes me want to stake the nearest vampire."

Marissa's jaw dropped open. "Britta! What about your sweater?"

Britta tossed the mess of yarn onto Marissa's lap. "A token of my appreciation for your patience with me." She grinned at me. "I'm outta here. Let's go, new witch."

CHAPTER 7

"So knitting was a dead end?" Gareth asked. He stood behind me as I prepared dinner, ready to offer what he deemed 'constructive criticism' and what I deemed 'annoying.'

"In more ways than one," I said. "I don't know how people do it. The needles, the yarn, the attention to detail." I gesticulated wildly.

"Take a deep breath and settle down," Gareth replied calmly. "Focus on the bigger issue. What did you learn?"

I took a moment to slow my heart rate. "I learned that Astrid's sister is a complete nut and Marissa is not the spell caster."

"I didn't think she was. She loves performing. I don't think she'd risk a prison sentence for a single role."

"You should have seen the parking lot, though," I said. "People seem to be getting out of hand, knowing that the council is out of commission."

Gareth reached for the knife, desperate to re-chop the carrots that I'd set aside. He hated when I sliced them crooked. He hated it even more when his hand ghosted right through the handle of the knife.

"We don't want Spellbound descending into lawlessness," he said. "Residents will only get more daring the longer the spell continues unabated. Someone needs to get to the bottom of this."

"I'm only one person," I said impatiently. "I'm doing the best I can."

Gareth shot me a sympathetic look. "I didn't mean you, Emma. No one expects you to solve this problem on your own. There are plenty of others to help."

I shook off the perceived criticism. I knew that came from years of living under the thumb of a tough grandmother.

"Yes, there are plenty of helpers," I said, eating my dinner at the kitchen counter. I'd made a habit of eating most meals here when I was without a living dinner companion. "No one likes seeing the council this way."

"Have you checked in the library for books of spells?" he asked. "If the dwarf can find the Endless Sleep spell in a library book, then perhaps you can find a way to reverse the youth spell."

"That's a good idea," I said. "What about the covens' grimoires?" When I met with the town librarian, she'd mentioned to me that each witch in the coven possessed a grimoire upon graduation from the academy, a book of spells. Maybe one of the more advanced witches had a grimoire that would be helpful.

"You should ask your kindly professor," Gareth said. "I'm sure someone keeps track of all the coven inventory."

"Good idea," I said. "He's probably the best person to ask about grimoires anyway." He was, after all, Lady Weatherby's second-in-command.

"Magpie spent a lot of time on the living room windowsill

today," Gareth said. "I think he was keeping an eye out for company."

"In a hopeful way?" I asked.

Gareth nodded. "I think you should invite another cat over soon."

"When this whole mess is over, I promise I will." I hesitated. "Octavia complained to me about shifters on their property ignoring the ordinances. Don't you think it's odd that the shifters were willing to break the law on the harpies' property, but not on ours?"

"Maybe thanks to your past good deeds, someone has set clear boundaries for the pack," Gareth said. "You know they like to operate differently from the rest of town."

I did help solve the murder of Alex's fiancée and he was a rising star of the pack. Still…

I regarded Gareth carefully. "Do you know something? Did you have the property warded?"

His expression remained blank. "I had nothing to do with it."

"Nothing to do with it implies something was done." I reached for his arm, but my hand went right through him. Apparitional advantage. "Gareth, if you know something, you have to tell me."

"I wouldn't feel right. It was clearly meant to be a secret."

Someone warded my property without telling me. Who would do that?

"Can you at least tell me what the ward does?" I asked.

He exhaled. "It's a protective ward. Keeps out undesirables. Anyone with intent to damage the property or harm you."

There was only one resident in Spellbound who cared enough about me to do a thing like that.

"Was it Daniel?"

Gareth pretended to zip his lip. "I'll take it to the grave."

"You're already in the grave."

"True, but I'm not a snitch."

"Sedgwick," I called. If my familiar knew the truth, he'd tell me. That was our bond.

Think again, came Sedgwick's reply. *Our bond means you feed me and I read your mind when you don't want me to.*

That's not a bond. That's an invasion of privacy.

You take what you can get.

"Fine. I'm going out now. Try not to let some mysterious figure redecorate my bedroom while I'm gone."

"Where are you off to?" Gareth asked.

"The Spellbound Care Home."

"You should be careful," he said. "You spend any more time there and they'll mistake you for a resident."

"I've got more than a few wrinkles to go," I said.

"What kind of mischief will Agnes be up to this evening?" Gareth asked.

"I'm not going to see Agnes specifically," I said. "There's an artist there tonight who was unhappy with the council and I'd like to talk to him after he's done finger painting with pudding or making macaroni art."

"What's his name?"

"Lachlan."

"Aye," he said. "I know Lachlan. Do go and enjoy some of his artwork. Let me know how it goes."

Once again, he seemed to know something that I didn't.

"Anything I need to know?" I asked.

Gareth smiled, showing his fangs. "All in good time."

I drove over to the Spellbound Care Home in time for Lachlan's art class. I pictured twenty elderly residents, paintbrushes in hands, trying to replicate bland landscapes and too-bright sunsets. Imagine my surprise when I entered the cafeteria and saw a huge canvas stretched out in the middle of the room with Agnes standing in the middle of it, stark naked.

I screeched to a halt and averted my gaze. "Holy Shar Pei. What's happening here?"

The pixie beside me giggled. "Nude body painting," she replied. "That's what Lachlan is famous for. Some of the residents have been begging for him to come. When his art project fell through with the town council, he finally said yes."

I watched as the incubus dipped his brush in gold paint and began to cover her saggy breasts with it.

"There. Are. No. Words," I said. "Is he going to paint a pastoral scene on her? I don't understand."

"Agnes specifically requested a gold body," the pixie replied. "But usually he prefers to let inspiration strike."

It was hard to imagine inspiration striking the incubus when standing in front of a body completely at the mercy of gravity. Even her wrinkles had wrinkles.

To my horror, Agnes caught sight of me and waved me over.

"You must remain still, Agnes," Lachlan said, in a tone highly suggestive of artistic temperament.

In the group of onlookers, I noticed a woman with a camera slung over her shoulders. Based on her chiseled cheekbones and sleek headscarf, I was going to go out on a limb and say this was Althea's sister, Miranda. She smiled when she saw me.

"You must be Emma Hart," she said, coming toward me. "I've heard so much about you from my sister."

"Miranda, right?"

She winked. "Eldest and wisest Gorgon."

"Did the care home hire you to take pictures today?" I asked.

"No, I work with Lachlan fairly often. Whenever he has an event or a custom piece, he calls me to take photos for posterity."

"I guess because he uses paint on people, it doesn't last."

"Exactly," she replied. "Once they get a bath or shower, the art is gone. That's what makes it so special."

Special. That was one word for it. I watched Agnes giggle as the paint bristles tickled under her arm. She was as giddy as a schoolgirl. It was equally charming and alarming.

"Do you happen to know anything about Lachlan's request to the council?" I asked. If they worked together a lot, he may have told her about the rejection.

She shushed me. "Don't even bring it up in front of him, especially now when he's working. He was very upset."

"How upset?"

Miranda lowered her voice. "He has a bit of a temper, you see. Part of his artistic nature. He was obsessed with his idea for a live show in the town square. He couldn't believe the council would reject it. To him, it's art in its purest form."

"But to the council, it was obscene?"

She pressed her lips together. "Not obscene necessarily. They just didn't want a bunch of naked residents in the town square. They didn't want to incite a riot."

The gentle sound of hissing reminded me of what was underneath her headscarf. Miranda's eyes rolled upward. "Pipe down, ladies. No one is talking to you."

I wondered if her relationship with her snakes was similar to my relationship with Sedgwick. Thank goodness the owl was not attached to my head. It was bad enough to have him flying over it.

Lachlan continued to work methodically over Agnes's body. I noticed Silas watching from the edge of the canvas, a naughty grin plastered across his face. I could only imagine the hijinks the genie and the old witch would get up to later.

I ripped the thought from my mind. My dinner hadn't yet digested and I didn't want to tempt fate.

"Does Lachlan dabble in magic at all?" I asked. As an incubus, his main focus was sexual expression. Vampires fed on blood, whereas Lachlan fed on sexual energy.

"I've never seen him use magic," Miranda said, and then hesitated. "That's not true actually. I've seen him use magic in a few of his exhibits. It adds flair to the artwork."

He should've used magic to paint Agnes. He was going to have to burn those brushes now.

"Were you with him when he heard the news about the council's veto?" I asked.

She nodded. "We were preparing for a different show. I haven't seen him that furious in a long time. I ended up with red paint on my headscarf." She touched the top of her head. "The girls were not happy. I can tell you that much."

"So the kind of magic he used for exhibits--did it involve spells?"

"More like fairy magic," she said. "Wandwork that added sparkles or illusions. Not your type of magic, if that's what you mean."

It was exactly what I meant. "Thanks, Miranda. That's really helpful."

Agnes seemed thrilled with her new golden body. I had to admit, his handiwork was impressive. She looked like she was wearing a gold bodysuit instead of paint.

"Now I want you to paint an arrow here," Agnes said, pointing to her lower abdomen.

"And what would you like it to say underneath?" Silas asked from the sidelines. "Open for business?"

"Only in your dreams," she snapped.

"Then I must have been dreaming a lot last night," he said with a smirk.

I wanted the chance to speak with Lachlan while he was

distracted. If he was involved in what happened to the town council, then I didn't want to give him a chance to formulate a story.

When Lachlan stopped to rinse off his brushes, I took the opportunity to test the waters.

"Impressive work, Lachlan," I said.

He regarded me with interest. "Thank you. I noticed you talking to Miranda. You're obviously too young to be a resident here."

"I volunteer here on occasion." I hesitated. "I think this would be an amazing project for the general population."

His expression clouded over. "So do I, but the council disagrees. A bunch of uptight troglodytes. I haven't been able to go anywhere near the Great Hall for a week for fear of attacking it with a paintbrush." His grip was so tight on the handle of the paintbrush that I worried he'd snap it in two.

"Really?" I said. "You've avoided the whole building?"

He gave a tense nod. "I need to renew my vehicle registration, but I'm waiting until my black mood passes. Who knows what I'll do if I see Lord Gilder's beady eyes on my way to the registrar's office? I don't trust myself."

"I think you made the right call," I said. Based on his response and body language, I was confident he wasn't our guy.

"If you'll excuse me, I need to move on to my next canvas," he said, then paused abruptly to appraise me. "If you're ever interested in working with me, I'd love to paint you."

I bet.

"Thanks, I'll think about it," I lied.

"I couldn't help but overhear your conversation," a familiar voice said.

I turned to see Silas. "Because you're nosy?"

He grinned. "I trade in information in here. Puddings for gossip. You know how it goes."

I really didn't, nor did I want to.

"I assume you're looking into the youth spell on the council," he said, wagging a finger at me. "Don't deny it. I know how you operate."

"I won't deny it," I said. "What can you tell me?"

"You should speak to Wilhelm Triers," Silas said. "He was my neighbor once upon a time and he was forever talking about something called chaos theory. I wouldn't be surprised if he could shed light on the current situation."

Chaos theory. Well, the town certainly had seen its share of chaos lately. Wilhelm was probably worth a brief conversation.

"Thanks, Silas," I said, and lowered my voice. "I'll make sure you get an extra pudding with tomorrow's dinner. I have connections, you know."

The genie nudged me with his elbow. "I do know. I may be old, but I'm not a fool, Emma."

"I never thought otherwise," I said.

CHAPTER 8

"I HAD a chance to speak with Edgar," I told Russ.

We sat in my office reviewing the latest information on his case. Despite the current state of the town council, the judge opted to go ahead with the trial since no one directly involved was impacted by the spell. It was the right decision, although I wouldn't have minded more time to prepare.

"And what did he say?" he asked.

"He believes that you didn't intentionally hit him and I'm sure he's willing to testify to that effect."

"That's good, right?"

"It will help." I threaded my fingers together. "One of the vampires seems to remember a genie called Brion in the pub."

Russ appeared thoughtful. "Yeah, I remember seeing him. Lanky fella with greasy hair."

"Samson believes that he may have deliberately redirected your bottle to hit Edgar. Samson saw his lips moving, like he was maybe doing an incantation."

Russ leaned forward, enthralled by this bit of news. "Why would he do that?"

"Apparently Edgar was responsible for having him kicked out of the country club. I'm going to speak with Brion myself. I just wanted to mention it to you first in case you knew anything about it."

"I don't." He broke into a wide grin. "Could this help let me off the hook? If he caused the bottle to hit Edgar?"

"Not entirely, but I might be able to argue for a lesser sentence because you lacked the necessary intent to hit Edgar."

He rubbed his hands together. "Nice one. I like a smart witch."

"Don't get too enthusiastic. I'm not making any promises."

"It's cool. I get it." He eyed me appreciatively. "You know, you should really hang out around the pack more often. I can name a dozen werewolves on both hands who'd love a crack at you."

A crack at me? Ugh.

"A dozen werewolves, Russ? On both hands?" I waited for the math to sink in, but it didn't happen. "I'm not really interested in dating right now, but thanks for thinking of me."

"Is this because of that vampire you went out with?" he asked. "If he's scaring you away from other dudes, just let me know and I'll…"

"Chuck a bottle at his head?" I interjected. "Demetrius isn't scaring anyone, Russ. And I'm a big girl. I'll handle my own business."

"Will you let me know when you talk to Brion?" he asked. His expression turned so hopeful and eager, I hated to let him down.

"I will."

He slapped his hands on the armrest and hopped to his feet. "Thanks, babe. You're awesome."

I opened my mouth to correct him, but he was out the door before I could form the words. Werewolf speed.

"Althea," I called, summoning the Gorgon to my office. It was time for the next item on my agenda.

She appeared in the doorway. "You rang, Your Ladyship?"

I groaned. "Now you sound like Sedgwick." The last thing I needed was another smartass in my life.

"I'm kidding," Althea said. "What do you need?"

"What do you know about the Grey sisters?" I asked.

Her snakes began hissing wildly and she placed her hands on the sides of her headscarf to calm them.

"The Grey sisters, huh?"

"You know them?" I asked.

Althea made a noise at the back of her throat. "More than I care to."

I gave her a quizzical look. "What are you not telling me?"

She heaved a sigh. "We're cousins. Some people mistakenly think we're half sisters, but we're absolutely not."

Wow. Althea was related to the Grey sisters. I couldn't decide whether this was good news or bad news.

"I need to go see them for Gareth," I said. "Maeve McCullen told us they can help him learn to become more active as a ghost."

Althea raised an eyebrow. "And he's sending you as his emissary? I thought he liked you."

I shrugged. "No choice. He can't venture to their cave in his condition."

"And you plan to convince one of them to make house calls?" Althea asked, and barked a deep, throaty laugh. "Good luck with that."

"I promised him I'd try," I said.

She blew out a breath. "Of course. Anything for Gareth." She pulled a chair closer to the desk and sat opposite me.

"Okay, if you want to get anywhere with those nasty cousins of mine, here's what you need to bring."

I grabbed my quill, ready for action. If a Gorgon tells you what to bring to appease her nasty cousins, you take copious notes.

"A headless chicken…"

I paused mid-stroke. "A what?"

"The sisters like their poultry."

"You mean plucked and wrapped in fairy paper, right?"

Althea gave me a no nonsense look. "What do you think?"

"Does it have to be headless?" I asked. "Can't they take care of that part?"

Althea folded her arms. "Do you want my help or not?"

I resumed writing. "Okay, okay. Continue."

"A jug of Goddess Bounty."

I'd never heard of that one. "Is it a type of wine?"

Althea laughed. "Oh, it's alcohol. Nothing as elegant as wine, though. And bring chocolate. They have a sweet tooth. I mean, they share it between them, but they have one."

"Anything else?"

"Your wand." She gave me a pointed look. "That's for your benefit. And have a few defensive spells on the tip of your tongue, just in case."

Her last suggestion made me uneasy. Were the sisters that dangerous?

"Maybe you should come with me," I suggested. "A little family reunion?"

The snakes hissed in response. "We're not particularly close. I don't think my presence would help you any. Might even be a hindrance."

My face fell. "What if they eat me?"

"With their one tooth and one eye between them? Highly doubtful." Althea stood and inclined her head. "Won't keep them from trying, though."

I groaned. Just another day in Spellbound.

I tracked down Brion at the less popular Windmill Golf Course on the eastern edge of town, past the Shamrock Casino. He'd just finished a game and was floating to his car, a bag of clubs slung over his shoulder. From the waist down, he reminded me of Silas. A small tornado in place of hips and legs.

"Excuse me. Are you Brion?"

He turned, scrutinizing me. "Do I know you?"

"Emma Hart, public defender." For a brief moment, I felt like I should be wearing a cape and a unitard.

"Oh, right. The new witch." He tossed the bag of clubs into the passenger seat of his car. "Can I help you with something?"

"I guess you've heard about Russ," I said.

"That he's a wereass?" Brion shrugged. "Not really news to me."

"That he's going on trial for aggravated assault," I corrected him. "You were at the Horned Owl that night, weren't you? I think I saw your name on the list of witnesses."

He nodded. "Saw the whole mess. That Russ should really curtail his drinking. All of those werewolves could stand to take it down a notch or two."

"And what about the vampires?" I asked. "Were they overindulging too?"

"No," he huffed. "They're too uppity to enjoy themselves like the werewolves. It's all pinkies out and perfectly tailored golf plaids."

So the werewolves were too wild, but the vampires were too 'uppity.' I wondered where witches fell on the Behavioral Scale According to Brion.

"Do you know Edgar, the victim?" I asked.

He snorted. "Of course. Edgar's got a stake shoved so far up his ass I'm surprised it hasn't pierced his heart."

"Really? What makes you say that?" I asked. "I've met him a handful of times and I've found him to be kind and considerate."

Brion snorted. "Because you're a potential source of food. He wants to lull you into a false sense of security."

My gut twisted at the idea that Edgar viewed me as food. I'd initially had the same concern about Demetrius. The more I came to know Gareth's friends, though, the more I knew that simply wasn't true.

"So how do you know Edgar?" I asked.

"He's a member of the Spellbound Country Club," he said. "He was always complaining to management about me so they finally revoked my membership."

"What was the basis of the complaint?" I asked.

Brion's face reddened. "He didn't think it was right for me to use magic on the course. I mean, he uses his vampire strength and reflexes. Why shouldn't a genie be able to use his natural skills?"

"I guess management saw it Edgar's way?"

"Yeah, sure, I mean the guy owns a piece of a successful blood bank and manages to roll in coins without lifting a finger. Of course management sided with him. The world isn't fair."

"No, Brion. The world isn't." Normal or paranormal, it was a tough lesson to learn. "I guess that makes you angry. The unfairness of it all."

"Damn straight."

"Angry enough to redirect the bottle thrown by Russ to make sure it hit Edgar?"

Brion balled his fists. "So what if I did? I didn't throw the bottle. The sheriff can't arrest me for anything."

O ye of little legal knowledge. "Actually, he can. In fact, there are several charges to choose from."

Brion seemed surprised. "What about Russ? He threw the bottle."

"And he will stand trial for that," I said. "But he may serve a lesser sentence if we can show that he didn't intend to hurt Edgar." I gave Brion a reproachful look. "And clearly he didn't."

Brion folded his arms and glared at me. "I'm not saying anything."

"Too late, Brion," I said, with a sympathetic smile. "I'm afraid you've already told me everything I need to know."

"I never thought we'd get that wand out of his nostril," Daniel said.

We were on our way back from babysitting Lord Gilder, Maeve, and Lady Weatherby and I was near exhaustion.

"It's my fault," I said. "I should have done a better job at hiding the wand. Lady Weatherby may have a child's mental state, but she's still clever."

"Oh, fabulous," a voice snapped. "Now my day simply cannot get any better."

An icy blond fairy gave us a look that would have frozen lava.

"It's good to see you, Elsa," Daniel said. "You're looking well, as always."

I stiffened. Elsa? Was this the daughter of Mayor Knightsbridge—the one Daniel had spurned? It had to be. She had her mother's fair complexion and even wore her blond hair in a similar fashion.

"Good to see me?" she repeated with a hollow laugh. "I'm pretty sure I told you the next time I saw you I wanted it to be facedown at the bottom of Tartarus."

"I think you may have said hell, but you made your point," he said good-naturedly.

She shoved her hands against her tiny hips. "I've heard you're trying to mend your ways, not that I'm keeping up with you in any way, shape, or form. I assume you're just working an angle we haven't figured out yet."

The angel shrugged. "No angle. Just want to make up for past transgressions."

She stopped and narrowed her eyes at me. "Can you believe the minotaur shit he's shoveling? The unicorn doesn't change its horn overnight, you know?"

"Not overnight," he said. "I think it's been a long time coming. It was really Emma who inspired me to move forward. To be a positive force in our tiny bubble of a world." He gave me an affectionate squeeze on the shoulder, which normally would make my heart thump wildly. The look on Elsa's face, however, stopped my heart in its tracks. The leveling expression gave even Lady Weatherby a run for her money.

"I can't take any credit, Daniel," I said. "Your good deeds are all down to you."

"Can one of your good deeds include removing the spell on my mother?" Elsa asked. "I can't take her like this. It was bad enough fighting with her before she aged backwards. This is far worse. It's like arguing with myself."

I noticed Daniel's lip twitch. Like he was desperate to smile but knew better.

"You had a fight with your mother before the spell took hold?" I asked. Was it possible she'd done the spell in anger and now had a change of heart but couldn't fix it? Elsa was a fairy, so she was capable of a wide variety of spells.

"Mother and I are always arguing about something," she huffed. "The last time it was over her lakeside cabin. I wanted to use it for a romantic getaway with my boyfriend." She shot a triumphant look at Daniel. "Yes, that's right. My very serious boyfriend, Jasper. He's the most wonderful man in Spellbound. No one else comes close."

"Congratulations," Daniel said. "I'm very happy for you."

That was not the response Elsa wanted to hear. I was fairly certain I saw steam come out of her ears.

"Anyway, Mother refused because she was planning to spend the weekend there with a few friends. It was ridiculous. She can use the cabin anytime she likes. Could she not make the occasional sacrifice for her only daughter?"

I had no horse in the race, but I did want to know more about the argument. "So what happened? The youth spell took hold before the weekend. Were you able to use the cabin?"

She smiled. "I suppose that is the one positive that came out of this mess. Jasper and I were able to enjoy ourselves at the cabin. But I need my mother back now." She even stomped her foot for good measure. If I hadn't known any better, I would have assumed she was under the spell as well.

"I think the entire town wishes the council would revert back to normal," I said. "It isn't just your mother who's been affected."

She flicked a dismissive finger in my direction. "Oh, I know that. The rest of it doesn't impact me, though. It's Mother who's driving me mad. If she borrows my clothes one more time, I'm going to have a complete meltdown."

"What kind of spell do you think was used?" I asked. "Everyone's calling it a youth spell." Maybe if I tested her knowledge, she would turn out to know more than an innocent person should.

"I have no clue," she said, pouting. "I didn't even know there was a spell like that or I might have used it on her ages ago. Now that I've seen the outcome, though, I wouldn't dream of it. She's a pain."

"I hear the sheriff is working hard to catch the spell caster," I said.

Elsa sighed. "Yes. Sheriff Hugo is a doll. I know he's doing everything in his power to help us."

Sheriff Hugo was a doll? So she was spoiled *and* delusional. Quite the combination. What had Daniel ever seen in her?

"Oh, look. There's my darling Jasper now. Gotta run." She gave Daniel a final glare before fluttering off to greet her boyfriend.

I waited a beat before addressing Daniel. "Elsa? Really?"

He gave me a rueful smile. "She's always been a spoiled brat," he said, "but I think that was part of her appeal. Plus, she always wore really short skirts. No one can argue with those legs."

"You really were shallow, weren't you?" It seemed so at odds with the deep thinker I knew.

"It was a phase." He paused. "A very long, disappointing phase."

"So do you think she had anything to do with the spell on the council?" I asked.

He stared after her as Jasper placed an arm around her and she whispered in his ear.

"Elsa's angry enough to pull a spell like that, but I don't think she's competent enough. She tried to curse me several times after we broke up, but all of them backfired."

"Backfired? How?"

He raked a hand through his mess of blond hair. "Let me think. One time, she tried to make me disgusting to all the women in town."

"How did it backfire?"

"It had the opposite effect," he said with a grin. "I suddenly became irresistible to every female in town. I had a line of ladies outside my door every morning for a week."

I smacked my forehead. "And I'm sure you handled that really well."

He grinned. "Elsa was apoplectic."

"But I thought you were already irresistible to the ladies of Spellbound. What effect would the spell have?"

"It deepened existing feelings," he explained. "Any woman who was already vaguely attracted to me suddenly found herself incredibly attracted to me. An enhancement."

I shook my head. "No wonder she hates you. And the mayor, too. You embarrassed them."

Daniel nodded sagely. "Humiliated them, really." He glanced back to the spot where Elsa had been standing. "Now that I think about it, I owe her a genuine apology."

"You're only realizing this now?"

"No, I've known for some time, but she hates me so much, I dread the thought of having the conversation."

"Maybe it's time for you to make a list of all the people you've wronged over the years and go and see them one by one to apologize."

"I predict a lot of doors slammed in my face," he said.

"That's okay," I said. "It's nice that you're volunteering and doing more community work, but if there are people still living in Spellbound who deserve an apology, then that might be a better use of your time."

He gazed at me with great affection. "You have a way of putting me on the right path, do you know that?"

My body pulsed with energy. I wished he wouldn't look at me like that. It wasn't fair. I didn't want to end up being a name at the bottom of his list of apologies.

I mustered my strength. "That's what friends are for."

CHAPTER 9

Despite my protests, Daniel insisted on accompanying me to the cave of the Grey sisters.

"You can't go and see them on your own," he said. "They would eat you alive."

I tried to use Althea's line of logic. "With what? The one tooth they share between them? I think I'll be fine."

"Even so, I'm coming. If nothing else, I'll carry the headless chicken." He grinned. "I consider it my good deed of the day."

I rolled my eyes. "You and your good deeds. Is there no end to them now?"

"I don't suppose you'd let me fly you to the cave," he said.

"No way," I said. "Sigmund will take us. I have directions."

"Then we should get going before it gets too close to sunset," he said. "A dark cave in daylight is bad enough. A dark cave in darkness is even worse."

I studied him. "Daniel Starr, are you afraid of three old women?"

"Let's review. Harpies, witches, Gorgons." He ticked them

off on each finger. "Grey sisters. Yes, I am emphatically afraid of the older women in this town."

I laughed to myself. "You're like the George Clooney of Spellbound."

He shook his head, confused. "Who's George Clooney?"

I patted him on the back. "Don't worry about it. Human reference."

We rode together in the green Volvo that Daniel had pulled from the bottom of Swan Lake and paid elves to magically enhance. It had been a thoughtful gesture, since this car was the last physical connection I had to my family.

"How far away from town do we need to go?" I asked. I couldn't read directions and drive at the same time. Not one of my skills.

"Out toward Curse Cliff," he said. "In the foothills, there are some caves. They live in the largest one."

I'd been to Curse Cliff recently, on a date with a werelion called Fabio. He freaked out when he found me standing on the cliff. Apparently, it was forbidden ground because it was allegedly the place from where the enchantress cursed the whole town and sealed the borders.

"Do you believe in the tale of Curse Cliff?" I asked.

Daniel cast a sidelong glance at me. "I didn't realize you knew the story."

"I've heard *a* story, but I don't know if it's *the* story. I stood on Curse Cliff and I felt nothing but peace and tranquility." It was true. I didn't feel any negative energy standing in the alleged spot.

We arrived at the mouth of the cave and I moved instinctively closer to Daniel. What was the etiquette for visiting a cave? Did we knock on this rock? Call in through the entrance?

Daniel was one step ahead of me. He cupped his hands

around his mouth and bellowed, "Good day, Grey sisters. You have visitors."

"They should really have a doorbell," I said. "This just makes it awkward for guests."

The sound of shuffling feet drew my attention to the darkened cave. An elderly woman emerged from the shadows, her white hair long and braided. She wore a brown cloak with a hood. Her one striking feature was her perfect nose. I would have expected something more prominent, but it was the nose I would have liked on my own face if given the choice.

"Who calls upon the Grey sisters?" she croaked. As she stepped into the light, I noticed her single eye for the first time. It was entirely white.

"I am Daniel Starr, accompanied by a young witch called Emma Hart."

She sniffed the air around us. "I know your name, Daniel Starr. Fallen angel that you are." She cackled softly. "A rhyme, don't you know? And a young witch on your arm, is it? So says you."

I inched closer to Daniel so that my hip was touching him.

"We came to ask for information," I said, trying to keep my voice from shaking. "We were told you might have the answers we seek."

She grinned and I saw nothing except her gums. "Who sent you?"

"The banshee, Maeve McCullen," I said. I omitted any reference to Althea since she didn't seem to think they would react positively to the Gorgon.

The sister nodded and motioned for us to follow. As she retreated further into the cave, I gave Daniel an uneasy look.

"It will be okay," he whispered, giving my hand a quick squeeze.

"We come bearing gifts," I said. We deposited the chicken and the jug of Goddess Bounty on the dirt floor in front of them.

"I smell chocolate," the tall sister said, inhaling deeply. "Where is it?"

"You'll get your chocolate when you've answered my questions."

"Oh?" the tall sister said. "So you do not intend to steal our eye and demand answers in exchange for its return?"

That seemed particularly cruel, considering they shared the one eye between the three of them.

"We have no interest in stealing your eye, thanks," I said. "We each have a set of our own."

The three sisters cackled and the sound bounced off the stark cave walls, adding to their eerie quality. They moved toward me, circling me one by one.

"You do not dance beneath the silvery moon," the short sister said. "Not one of them. Not one of them at all."

"Oh, I know," I said. "But they've allowed me into the coven since I am a witch, as long as I can meet the requirements."

They laughed again and I bristled.

"I know I'm not the best student, but I do think I'll pass all the classes…eventually."

"You have no tolerance for flight," said the middle one.

"And surely you have glimpsed what hides in dark corners," said the tall one.

The short one stood behind me and yanked up my hair. "She bears the mark," she cried.

The other two hurried to catch a glimpse.

"Give me the eye," the middle one insisted. I felt their elbows jostling each other.

"My turn now," said the tall one.

"Leave her alone," Daniel said firmly. "It's only a birthmark." He was the one who'd drawn my attention to it. Because the birthmark was at the nape of my neck beneath the hairline, I didn't know it was there until he told me.

The short one released my hair and I quickly stepped away from them.

"Not just a birthmark," the short one said.

"Do you know what it means?" I asked. "Do you know which coven I belong to?"

The short one held out her hand. "The chocolate."

I pulled a bar from my cloak pocket and handed it to her. Daniel came to stand beside me as the short sister tore the wrapper from the chocolate and breathed in its scent.

"It has been too long," she said, and opened her mouth to take a bite, which is when I made my move. I swooped in and snatched the tooth right out of her mouth. Her gums closed on the chocolate and she wailed in protest.

"I need my sweet tooth," she cried.

"Not until you tell me about my coven," I said. Never mind that I was here to ask about Gareth. If these sisters had information on my origin, I needed to know. Now.

The middle one stared at me through the single eye. "She is most determined, sister. And we know what she is, what she is capable of. For that alone, we would do best to answer."

What I was capable of? Right now the only thing I was capable of was not puking in my mouth while holding the old ladies' tooth. I'd never been a fan of the Tooth Fairy, coming to take the teeth of children in the middle of the night. I mean, for what purpose? I remembered crying every time I lost a tooth because I hated the blood and saliva that accompanied it.

"If I answer, you will return the tooth unharmed," the short one said.

"Of course," I replied.

"You cannot find your coven because you do not have one," she said.

"But all witches have covens," I insisted. "That's what everyone said."

"Witches do not fear heights," the tall one said. "But you do."

"Witches have feline familiars," the middle one said. "But not you."

The short one gave me a look that could only be described as sympathetic. "You must follow that logic to its natural conclusion."

Daniel spoke first. "Are you saying she's not a witch?"

"Of course I am," I said. "That's why I'm stuck here. I drank the potion that Ginger gave me and it made me glow purple."

"An easy mistake," the short one said. "As you are closely related."

What was closely related to a witch? I glanced helplessly at Daniel, whose turquoise eyes widened.

"No," he said. "It isn't possible."

"What isn't possible?" I asked. "Someone please tell me in plain English."

Daniel shook his head in disbelief. "I think what they're trying to say is that you're a...a sorceress."

My laughter echoed in the cave. "How can I be a sorceress?" I wasn't even sure I knew what a sorceress was.

"You are kissed by starlight," the tall one said. "The sign of the sorceress."

I touched the mark on the back of my neck. "What does that mean?"

"Black magic resides in you," the middle one hissed. "Very dark."

I tried to process what they were telling me. "And this is why I can see Gareth and Raisa's ghosts?"

"As one who is close to darkness, you are privy to much and more," the tall one said.

I didn't feel very close to darkness. Heck, I still preferred a nightlight.

"What about my owl?" I asked. "Is an owl familiar a sorceress thing?" Dark magic would certainly explain Sedgwick's salty attitude.

"The choosing is mutual," the short one said. "Any animal would do. A sorceress has no ties to a particular creature."

I began to feel dizzy as the enormity of their revelation settled over me. What did this mean? Would they kick me out of the academy? Banish me to some remote area of Spellbound?

"What exactly is the difference between a witch and a sorceress?" I asked.

"They are carved from the same mold," the middle one said. "But darkness calls to those kissed by starlight. Black magic."

"But I don't know any black magic," I insisted. "Doesn't that make me a witch?"

"It is not what you know," the tall one said.

"It is what you harbor inside you," the short one finished for her.

"Am I...evil?" I asked. I certainly didn't feel evil. Maybe Magpie would disagree, but I generally considered myself to be a nice person.

It was the only question they didn't answer.

"And what about my mother?" I asked. "Was she a sorceress too?"

"But of course," the tall one said. "Inherited magic is the most powerful."

My mother was the sweetest woman who ever walked the planet. No way was she inherently evil, nor was I.

"Why do you know this when no one else does?" I asked,

my irritation showing. "I consulted books, the coven. I even went to see Raisa." Visiting the frightening witch with a bone fence and iron teeth was not an experience I cared to repeat.

"They have forgotten the world that we once belonged to," the tall one said. "Trapped too long in one place, they have been."

"The eye sees more than what is in front of it," the short one added. "Now return the tooth. We have more than held up our end of the bargain."

I couldn't argue with that.

"You know, I've noticed at least three dentists in town," I said. "Have you considered paying one of them a visit? I'm pretty sure you could each have your own set of teeth if you were so inclined."

The three sisters exchanged surprised glances.

"You seriously never thought of that?" I rolled my eyes. "And people here think I'm ignorant. I mean, if we can put a man on the moon, I bet the optometrist can do something about your eyesight, too. She's a fairy, for crying out loud." I folded my arms and assessed them. "I'll make you a deal. One of you agrees to help my friend Gareth improve his ghosting skills and I'll set you up with a new set of chompers."

"Leave the cave?" the short one asked, uncertain.

"I'm afraid so," I said. "Gareth's movements are restricted. I'll handle the transportation, though. You just have to agree to come along."

The middle one stepped forward. "Lyra will go forth. A break from this hovel is much needed."

"Hovel?" the tall one shot back. "Our cave is wondrous. More hospitable it would seem if you cared for it.

"You should feel blessed by the gods to have a roof over your head," the short one added.

"A cold, stone roof with damp walls and two joyless

sisters for company," the middle one said. "Yes, how fortunate I am."

"Lyra is free to join you now," the short one said. "We have no tolerance for her today."

The middle one scowled at her sister.

Oh no. We couldn't take her now. "Let me make arrangements with the dentist first. That way you know I'm going to make good on my promise. I'm inherently evil, remember? I might try to double-cross you."

The middle one recoiled slightly. "As you desire. Send your owl with the time and place."

"Only if you promise not to eat him." Crap. Did I say that out loud? "I'll be in touch."

I hurried out of the cave with Daniel right beside me. Neither of us wanted to linger there one second longer than necessary. Even with a single tooth, I had the feeling the Grey sisters would be more than willing to make a meal of us.

CHAPTER 10

I WAS STILL REELING from the news on the ride home from the cave.

"So was it a sorceress that cursed the town?" I asked. "Am I like her?"

"An *enchantress* allegedly cursed the town," Daniel corrected me.

"Argh." I gripped the wheel in frustration. "So what's the difference between those two?"

"They're both in the same paranormal family tree as witches," Daniel said. "But an enchantress is often a beautiful woman who uses white magic."

"And I'm the ugly, evil one whose heart is made of black magic?" My jaw tensed. "That's so racist."

Daniel smiled. "No one said you were ugly, Emma."

"But I *am* evil, apparently."

He covered my hand with his. "And I'm a fallen angel. Together, we make quite a pair."

I tried to ignore the tingling in my body when his skin met mine. This was not the time to pine after Daniel, not when I needed to process everything I'd learned today.

"So here's what I don't understand," I said. "How can an enchantress have cursed the town? Doesn't that make her bad and, therefore, a sorceress?"

"I guess it depends on which version of the story you believe," Daniel said. "If she was someone in need of shelter and cursed us when we refused her hospitality, then she was trying to teach us a lesson. That's not necessarily black magic. In her mind, we were the bad ones and she was showing us the better path."

I lifted an eyebrow. "Everyone in town? For all eternity? Seems way harsh."

"Maybe, but still not dark magic."

I gave him a pointed look. "By all accounts, you were around then. Possibly even connected to the curse. Which version do you believe?"

He leaned back in the seat and closed his eyes. "I knew this conversation would have to happen sooner or later."

I tried to keep my eyes on the road, but all I wanted to do was look at Daniel. "You can tell me anything. You know that." *And it won't change the way I feel about you.*

He opened his eyes and blew out a breath. "Yes, there was a time when I got involved with someone of great power."

"Someone who answered to the name 'enchantress'?"

"She was called Lia."

"For how long?"

"In the grand scheme of things, not long at all. She was passing through town on her way to the west coast. She was beautiful and radiated power and confidence." He shrugged. "We hit it off."

"And?" I prompted. "What did you do to her?"

"I suppose I deserve the negative assumption," he said. "I grew tired of her rather quickly. Too much power and confidence are a dangerous combination, even in someone who isn't inherently evil."

"So where's Lia now? If you don't think she's the one who cursed the town, shouldn't she be trapped here?"

"I don't know," he said softly. "I assumed she left town before the curse took hold, not because she created it, though. That part was a coincidence."

"If you saw her again tomorrow, what would you say to her?" I asked. "Do you regret how you treated her?"

"Of course I do," he said. "I regret how I treated all of them. Sometimes I think of how I would feel if a man treated you the way I treated them and it makes my blood boil."

"Really?" My pulse began to race.

"I feel protective of you," he said. "It's my fault you're here, after all."

My heart grew heavy. Of course it was the guilt talking. I should have known.

"Speaking of that," I said. "You didn't have to ward my property. I appreciate it and all, but I can take care of myself."

Daniel looked at me askance. "What are you talking about?"

"The protective spell around my yard to keep out the bad elements," I said. "Wasn't that you?" I'd been certain Daniel was the culprit.

He shook his head. "I'm sorry to say it wasn't. I guess someone else is looking out for you."

How about that?

"Emma," Daniel said carefully. "About the sorceress thing…I don't think we should tell anyone about what we learned in the cave."

"Why not?"

"I…I'm not sure how people would feel," he said. "I think they might treat you differently."

"Differently how?"

"Like someone capable of horrible atrocities."

Oh.

"So we're going to keep it a secret?" I asked. I wasn't a fan of secrets. In my experience, secrets seemed to rot and fester.

"I think it's a necessity." He patted my knee. "To keep you safe."

"Do you think the coven would disown me?" I asked.

"Possibly. Lady Weatherby is quite strict. It was a miracle she agreed to take you under her wing, knowing you weren't one of theirs."

I knew he was right. I pictured myself moving into Raisa's isolated cottage in the forest with its bone fence and jars of live mice. No thank you.

"If that's what you think is best," I said, "then let's keep it between us."

"At least we trust each other," he said. "I'm relieved I decided to come with you."

Me too. For more reasons than I was willing to say.

"I'm glad I have you, Daniel. Sometimes I don't know what I'd do without you."

He smiled. "Let's never find out."

I found Wilhelm Triers behind the house where he was tending to his garden. He was tall and thin, with a shock of white hair and limbs like rubber.

"You grow all these yourself?" I asked, admiring the variety of plants and flowers in one small space.

"I do." He stopped trimming and looked at me. "I would say that I don't allow unsolicited visitors, but I get the distinct impression that you're not here to sell me something."

"No, definitely not," I said, with a self-deprecating laugh. "I couldn't sell blood bags to a mob of hungry vampires."

"Speaking of hungry…" He glanced above our heads. "Your owl seems in need of a snack. Tell him there are plenty of voles in the copse back there." He gestured to an area beyond the backyard.

Sedgwick, this guy is looking out for you, I said. *Voles at twelve o'clock.*

That or he's trying to get rid of any potential witnesses.

I glared at him. *Stop trying to scare me.*

He chuckled and flew off. What did I ever do to deserve a smartass owl?

"I'm Emma, by the way. You're Wilhelm, right?"

"I am." He removed his gardening gloves and shook my hand. "What can I do for you?"

"Silas suggested I speak with you."

His expression brightened. "How is dear Silas? Such a wonderful neighbor for so many years."

"He's well. Loves life in the care home." With all the tail he was chasing, why wouldn't he? "You don't visit him?"

"Not as often as I should," he admitted.

"He said you might have thoughts about the craziness that's been happening around here."

"When you say craziness, I assume you're referencing the recent spell on the town council?"

"I am."

"I understand that Sheriff Hugo wasn't affected," he said. "Are you here at his behest?"

"No, I'm here as the public defender," I said.

"Though you have no official investigative role?" he queried.

"Sort of an all hands on deck situation," I said. And Sheriff Hugo was taking his sweet time as always.

Wilhelm clucked his tongue. "Sheriff Hugo. How long will we put up with his ineptitude? We get the leaders we deserve, I suppose."

Good to know we agreed that the sheriff was inept, however, I wasn't sure that the town deserved him. It was only thanks to his personal relationships with key power players in town that they were stuck with him.

"Tell me, Emma, are you familiar with chaos theory?" he asked.

"Only what Jeff Goldblum told me."

He gave me a blank look. I guess he'd never heard of a little movie called Jurassic Park. Too bad. He was missing out.

Wilhelm shook his head before returning to his regularly scheduled diatribe. "It is a branch of mathematics. I like to refer to it as surprise science."

"That sounds adorable."

"Adorable, yes." He began to walk through the garden and motioned for me to join him. "The systems in our world are complex and, therefore, difficult to understand. Chaos theory deals in such matters."

"Have you ever wanted to test the theory?" I asked. "Maybe cause a bit of chaos and confusion in Spellbound and gauge the results? Can't say I'd blame you. Same thing day after day, knowing there's no hope of significant change…" I trailed off, hoping he'd bite.

"Oh, I don't know about that," he said, with an air of mystery.

I squinted. "What don't you know?"

A slow grin spread across his face. "Well, your presence in town was rather a surprise, wasn't it? One might even argue that you, Emma Hart, are an agent of chaos."

"One could argue it, but one would lose." I didn't like the idea of being an agent of chaos. I liked to think I solved problems, but a label like that made me feel like I caused them instead.

He patted his brow with a plaid handkerchief. "You, my dear, were impossible to predict and have proven difficult to control." He chuckled softly. "You are the epitome of the infinite complexity of nature."

"So you're telling me, unequivocally, that you had no hand in the youth spell," I said. Right to the point this time.

"None at all," he replied. "Although, I'll admit, it's been fascinating to watch from an academic point of view. Unlike others in Spellbound, I've learned to expect the unexpected."

"I'm surprised how quickly people are acting out," I said. "Refusing to follow the rules. Mistreating one another. It's getting ugly out there."

"Perhaps I should spend more time in town than I typically do," he said, with a trace of amusement. "It isn't often that I'm treated to such a spectacle. The heavy hand of bureaucracy keeps residents in line most of the time."

"Do you have any idea who might be responsible?" I asked. "Have you heard any gossip or know of anyone unhappy with the council?"

"Not that I indulge in idle gossip," he said, "but perhaps you should pay a visit to Janis Goodfellow. The last time I ran into her at the Enchanted Garden, she was furious that the council had refused permission for her to plant nightshade and hemlock."

Interesting. Janis was one of the names mentioned in the council minutes. "Those are poisonous, right?"

"Very."

"Then I can understand the council's refusal."

He shrugged. "She is an herbologist. She feels it is her nature-given right. I can't say that I disagree."

"So if she's an herbologist, does that make her a witch?"

"It does, indeed." He clapped me on the shoulder. "Not to worry, Emma. I have every confidence you'll meet the other members of your adopted coven in due time. You are, after all, such a novelty. They'll all want to meet you sooner or later."

I didn't want them to meet me because I was a novelty. I wanted them to meet me because they were genuinely interested in me. Just like I wanted someone like Demetrius to want to date *me*, rather than date the new curiosity in town.

"Thanks for your time, Wilhelm. I appreciate you answering my questions."

"Anything for Silas."

"So based on your chaos theory, how do you predict this whole thing will play out?"

He gave me a mischievous wink. "Everyone will live happily ever after."

CHAPTER 11

As WILHELM'S house faded from view, I mulled over our conversation. Was I really an agent of chaos? I'd only tried to be helpful since my arrival in town. Even though I grew impatient at times with Spellbound's bureaucracy, I had no interest in dismantling it. Not completely, anyway. Just a little reform.

Look out, Sedgwick screeched from his position above the car.

I hit the brakes and narrowly avoided a collision with an enormous wolf.

How could you not see the giant mammal in front of you? he scolded me.

I got out of the car to make sure the wolf was uninjured. By the time I made it to the front, the wolf had shifted to human form.

"Alex," I exclaimed.

The rising leader of the werewolf pack jumped to his feet, completely naked.

"What are you doing running around as a wolf in broad daylight?" It seemed that everyone was indulging in rule breaking now that the council was preoccupied with mud pies and dodgeball.

"Tracking your scent," he said. "I need you to come with me."

A hot, naked werewolf was demanding that I accompany him. Somehow, it wasn't as sexy as it should have been.

"What's going on?" I asked.

"It's the council."

Of course it was.

"They've taken over the bounce houses. Kicked out all the children. Markos isn't sure how to handle it and he can't reach the sheriff."

"And you think I can do something?"

"Lucy mentioned that you have a knack for handling them. I thought we might manage to wrangle them if we work together."

I glanced down at his exposed parts. "I'm not sure how the immature version of the council will respond to the sight of a naked man giving them orders."

Alex grimaced. "I raced out of the house in wolf form as soon as the message from Markos arrived. I didn't plan ahead."

"Get in the car," I said. I wasn't excited about the idea of a bare werewolf butt on my upholstery, but I refused to complain. "We'll swing by a shop on the way into town and grab you clothes."

"Can't you do a clothing spell or something?" he asked, sliding into the passenger seat.

I laughed. "You grossly overestimate my abilities, Alex."

We sped into town, ignoring speed limits and other traffic signs and I realized I was as guilty of ignoring the rules as anyone else. If we weren't careful, the entire infrastructure of the town could unravel.

I parked in the first available spot and hurried from the car.

"You run into Ready-to-Were and get Ricardo to help you. Meet me at the bounce house."

He left the car and immediately shifted back into wolf form to preserve his modesty. He took off toward the town square and I ran toward the bounce house.

The scene was chaotic when I arrived. There were actual children huddled off to the side, wailing to their parents. An attractive man stood in front of the giant inflatable bounce house, trying to speak in a reasonable tone to the group inside. I saw Mayor Knightsbridge push Lord Gilder against the wall. He bounced off the side and fell flat on his bottom. His fangs sprang to life, but the mayor was too quick for him. She froze him with her wand before he could move.

"How did she get her wand back?" I asked aloud.

"She's the mayor," the man said. "If she wants something, she makes it happen, even in her childlike state."

"Where's Markos?" I asked, craning my neck for the sight of the minotaur. I figured he'd be hard to miss. "Alex said he's the one who sent a message for help."

"I'm Markos," the man said.

I scrutinized him. He was far too good-looking to be a hideous minotaur. He was very tall—about six and a half feet —with broad shoulders and bulging muscles where I didn't know muscles existed.

"But you look…" I faltered.

His mouth quirked. "Human? That's the idea. I have a human form and my natural form."

"Like a shifter?" I queried.

"More like the harpies. Our human forms are the result of magic. I drink a custom tonic. I get fewer odd looks in this body, so I tend to prefer it." He grinned. "Plus, this body fits in my car."

I was willing to bet he got a lot more appreciative looks in this body as well. It was hard not to stare. I struggled to focus on the task at hand.

"So you're having a bit of trouble with the council?" I asked.

"They've frightened away the children and are wreaking havoc in there," he said. "I've thought about changing to my minotaur form and scaring them, but I don't want to overdo it. They're childlike, but they still have their mature magic and abilities. If Lorenzo attacks me in his wolf form, it's going to be a problem."

"I'm here," Alex said. "What can I do?"

I whipped around and was relieved to see him fully clothed, although I resisted the urge to smile at the outfit. He wore a turquoise shirt with white polka dots and bright white trousers. Not Alex's usual hillbilly style.

"Did Ricardo not let you choose your own clothes?" I asked. When it came to fashion, Ricardo had what I called flair.

"He said it would be faster if he did it," Alex replied.

Right.

"So what's the plan?" Markos asked.

Lord Gilder was now crying and screaming for mercy, pinned beneath Wayne's wide troll body.

Alex folded his arms and watched with amusement as Juliet bounced straight up and hit her head on the ceiling. The Amazon was far too tall for bouncing.

"Would it be wrong to record any of this first?" Alex asked. "Just for laughs later on."

"They would kill you in your sleep and hide the evidence," Markos said.

A forlorn Maeve sat on the edge of the bounce house, swinging her heels against the side. I decided to start with her.

LUCKY CHARM

"Maeve, is everything okay?" I asked, moving to sit beside her.

The banshee sniffed. "I wanted to play with Lady Weatherby, but she said I couldn't play with her because I smelled like death."

"Well, that was mean, wasn't it?"

Maeve nodded, fighting an onslaught of tears. "She's always mean. She and the mayor are such bullies."

I placed an arm around her. "You're very special, Maeve, and everyone likes you. Nobody thinks you smell like death." Whatever that meant. "Never mind what the mean girls say to you."

Maeve looked at me, tears dangling from her thick eyelashes. "You're the nicest girl in Spellbound."

"Oh, I don't know about that," I said. "I have my moments, same as anyone else."

"Do you want to have a tea party with me?" she asked, her expression hopeful.

"Um, I'd love to, but I have to help my friend Markos right now."

Maeve cocked her head, eyeing the minotaur. "All of the ladies in town think he's a real catch. I think he's too tall and hairy."

I patted her knee. "You never know. You might like that when you're older."

"What kind of help does he need?"

"To be honest, he needs you and your friends to leave the bounce house. He has paying customers who were a little intimidated by your group."

She giggled. "I guess we are bigger than the other kids."

"You know them better than anybody," I said. "Can you think of a way to get them to listen?"

Her lips curled into a smile. "As a matter of fact, I do. You might want to cover your ears, though."

103

I held my hands over my ears and moved back toward Markos and Alex. Maeve opened her mouth and let loose a wailing cry that shook me to my core. The keening continued until every council member dropped to his or her knees.

Maeve dusted off her hands. "Mission accomplished."

I stepped toward the bounce house. "Listen up, council members. Playtime is over for today. Lorenzo, you're going to go with Alex to the Pines, where the pack can look after you. Lady Weatherby, you come with me to the coven. Lord Gilder, you're going to wait here for Demetrius. Mayor Knightsbridge, you're going to wait for Lucy. Markos will look after the rest of you until your loved ones can come and claim you."

Markos laid a firm hand on my shoulder. "Well done, Emma. Alex was smart to find you."

"I helped him once before," I said. I saved him from a psychopathic werewolf who'd killed his fiancée, Jolene.

His expression darkened. "Yes, poor Jolene. A tragedy."

"I guess Alex felt he could trust me after that."

"And his trust was well placed. No one can argue with a werewolf's instincts."

"You don't mind keeping an eye on the rest of the kids until someone picks them up, do you?"

"Not at all." He smiled down at me and his brow furrowed. "Are you making fun of me?"

"Huh?" I quickly understood when I felt the stiffness in my cheeks. I was grinning back at him like a lunatic. The smile faded. "No, sorry. Of course not."

Lady Weatherby came and stood beside me. "Can we go now? How about now?" She poked my arm with her wand and I snatched it. "Hey!"

"You're not supposed to have access to magic right now," I said. "Coven's orders." The mayor and Lady Weatherby seemed to have spare wands stashed all over town. It was like playing whack-a-wand.

She began to pout. "Killjoy."

"Trust me. It's for your own good." And everyone else's.

Janis Goodfellow was on her hands and knees in the dirt, bottom high in the air.

I cleared my throat. "Hello, I'm..."

She flipped over and peered up at me, shielding her eyes from the sun. "Yes, yes. Emma Hart. New witch on the block. Yada yada. I know."

"You recognize me?"

She pointed skyward. "Your owl gave you away. I saw his shadow pass overhead a couple of minutes ago. Reconnaissance, was it?"

"Sedgwick likes to check things out for me," I admitted. Plus, he's nosy.

She stood and dusted the dirt from her knees. "So how can I help you, newbie?"

"You can call me Emma. I came to talk to you about your dispute with the town council."

"Why?" she asked with a note of eagerness. "Do you need nightshade? Or maybe a little belladonna?"

"No, no. I'm not interested in any deadly plants." With my luck, I'd accidentally poison my entire harp therapy group. Wouldn't Sheriff Hugo love the opportunity to arrest me for mass murder?

She arched an eyebrow. "Not interested? Darling, you're a witch. You should want to learn everything there is to know."

"I don't think poisonous plants are covered in this year's curriculum." Truth be told, I had no idea what the rest of the school year entailed. Somehow, I couldn't see Lady Weatherby trusting the remedial witches with deadly...

anything. We were still in the training wheels phase of our education.

"It wasn't like that back when Agnes was in charge," she complained. "We learned by trial and error. None of this classroom malarkey."

"Were you at the academy when Agnes was head of the coven?"

Her head bobbed. "The academy was less formal then. None of these certificates and other nonsense. If you lived, you passed."

The tough love approach.

"So what do you want to know about the dispute?" she asked.

I took a careful step away from the vines brushing against my arm. It seemed I couldn't be too careful in this garden.

"It's my understanding that you requested permission to include certain deadly plants in your garden that are generally prohibited."

"That's right and the council denied the request." She bristled. "Lady Weatherby, head of the coven. You would think she of all people would approve it."

"Were you angry?"

Her hands moved to her hips. "Of course I was angry. I'm an herbologist who's restricted from keeping important plants in my garden. It's an outrage. No one tells the mixologist not to keep certain cocktails in her bar. Does anyone tell you that you can't keep certain law books in your office?"

"To be fair, my law books can't kill anyone."

"Hit 'em hard enough in the head with one and we'll see about that."

I swallowed hard. Note to self: never invite Janis to my office.

"What did you do when you found out your request was denied?" I asked.

Janis looked thoughtful. "I dropped by to see the Minors. They're always willing to lend a sympathetic ear when it comes to council matters."

Or eat one.

"Did they offer any advice?" I asked. Like seek revenge with a magic spell.

"No," she replied. "Just a cup of tea and delicious sandwiches. I'm still angry about it, to be honest. I'm a member of her own coven and she failed to support me."

Time to trot out the truth for Janis. "Actually, it says in the council minutes that she voted in favor of you."

"She what?" Janis hesitated and the color rushed to her cheeks. "Oh."

"She wasn't the only one either, although the majority did rule against you." But together they put up a united front. The town council could give lessons on good parenting.

"I...That's good to know." She stared blankly at the berries in her basket. "I just assumed…"

"Do you know anything about the youth spell?"

"Is that why you're here?" she asked, her voice rising. "You think I was seeking revenge?"

"We're working our way through all the recent requests that came before the council and were denied," I said diplomatically. "You were on the list."

Janis laughed. "Trust me, darling. If I were going to get revenge, the last thing I would do is cast a spell that let's them relive their glory days. I don't know who did it, but I can tell you that the responsible party wasn't trying to punish them."

"You don't think?" I said. "Not even to make fools of them?"

She slapped her knee. "Are you kidding? They're having the time of their lives. The culprit did them all a favor with this spell. They're an uptight bunch of bureaucrats, especially that Mayor Knightsbridge, but they're running around town with lollipops and singing songs. Every new day is pure joy."

Janis made a good point. Every time I saw them, they were having fun, which didn't seem like punishment at all. Food for thought.

"Thank you, Janis. You've been really helpful."

"If you decide you'd like to know more about herbology," she said, "feel free to come and see me. You and your friends. There's a lot I can teach you, with or without my deadly garden."

Let's go, Sedgwick urged. *Her cat is giving me serious side eye.*

I glanced to my right to see a tuxedo cat staring up at him.

"That's Bella," Janis said. "She doesn't like owls. Whenever a message arrives, the owls know to drop it at the end of the driveway before Bella catches wind of them."

"I guess you don't keep a messenger owl then."

"Heavens no. I use Elf Express. Very reliable and convenient. No mess to clean up."

I'm a grown owl. No one cleans up after me, Sedgwick objected.

It's nothing personal, I told him. *Not everyone likes owls the same way not everyone likes cats.*

Well, I can understand not liking cats. They're horrid creatures.

I smiled to myself. Grumpy or not, the owl was definitely my familiar. With a final wave, Sedgwick and I left the garden and headed home.

CHAPTER 12

"Stars and stones, he was on the toilet!"

I laughed at Begonia's reaction when the T-Rex ate the lawyer. My recent visit with Wilhelm prompted me to introduce the other witches to Jurassic Park in the remedial witch hideout, our secret place away from the watchful eyes of the coven. Professor Holmes had cancelled class, so we were able to enjoy an afternoon movie for a change.

"Shit happens," Millie said, and laughed at her own joke.

Sophie cast a sidelong glance at me. "Are you even watching?"

"I've seen it more times than I can remember," I said.

"And you're thinking about the youth spell," Millie said. "I'm starting to recognize your expressions. This one is frustration mixed with determination."

"I think you have an untapped talent," I told Millie. Now that I'd dismissed every suspect on the list, I needed a new theory.

"You're out of leads?" Begonia asked, her gaze still pinned to the magic mirror that doubled as a screen.

"Janis was right," I said. "This spell isn't about revenge.

And Wilhelm doesn't think it's purely to cause chaos, and it isn't a coup because no one has tried to take over the leadership role."

"So what does that leave?" Sophie asked.

"Well, the person who performed the spell has to be somewhat experienced," Millie said. "There's no way someone could put a spell on the Great Hall without a strong magical background."

"And the registrar's office," Sophie added. "Poor Stan. Talk about the wrong place at the wrong time. You can relate to that, Emma."

I sat silently for a moment, an idea beginning to flicker. "Maybe we've been coming at this from the wrong angle. What if he wasn't in the wrong place at the wrong time? What if it was the council in the wrong place at the wrong time?" Excitement grew within me. "What if the person wasn't as experienced as we think and they accidentally put a spell on the council when they only meant to use it on the registrar?" If the town council wasn't the intended target, then that would explain why our leads were all dead ends.

Begonia wrinkled her nose. "Why would someone want the registrar to have the mental state of a child?"

I snapped my fingers. "A distraction. They didn't want to hurt the registrar, only make sure that he couldn't interfere in whatever the spell caster was trying to achieve."

Millie perked up. "And the registrar controls all of the town's important documents. Licenses, leases, deeds, wills."

"Let's go to the registrar's office and see what paperwork was handled on the day the spell was cast," I said.

"But he's still a child," Begonia said. "Who's running the office?"

"Astrid, most of the time," I said. "She won't object to letting us snoop around."

Sophie glanced at the clock. "We should go now or the office will be closed."

Begonia looked longingly at the magic mirror. "Tell me now. Does the T-Rex die?"

"No spoilers," I said. "We'll watch the rest later."

Reluctantly, she followed us out the hidden door of the hideout.

Astrid was in the middle of locking up the office when we arrived.

"Wait," I called.

She stopped mid-turn and glanced over her shoulder. "What's up, witches? Wanna head over to the Horned Owl after my shift? They're hosting a new band tonight."

"Actually, we need to get into the office," I said. "Would you mind staying open a few extra minutes?"

She gave me a curious look. "A lead?"

"Maybe."

Hurriedly, she removed the key and stepped aside. "Have at it, ladies. Anything to end this nightmare."

We entered the office and went behind the counter to the room where all of the documents were stored. File cabinets and shelves were everywhere I looked.

"This is going to take hours," I said. "We need to find all the documents signed by the registrar the date the spell was cast." I didn't even know where to begin. Nothing appeared to be marked with dates.

"We don't need to look through the paperwork, silly," Begonia said. "We can do a spell."

"A spell?" I echoed. "To find paperwork?"

"Of course," Millie said, and produced her wand. "Allow me." She pointed her wand toward the file cabinets and said,

"Let's not leave this up to fate/show us documents with the relevant date."

Drawers slid open and papers floated through the air, landing on the table in front of us in neat piles.

"Holy Order and Efficiency," I whispered. "Every office in America could use a spell like that."

"I'll start with this stack," Sophie said, and began rifling through the documents in front of her. "These are all licenses."

"Mine are wills," Begonia said.

The first one in my pile was a property deed. "I guess this is my chance to dabble in real estate." My grandmother had tried to get me interested in real estate when I was younger. She loved watching the various property shows on television. Buying, selling, renovating—if it involved a house, then she was going to watch it.

Millie read out her first document, a lease renewal for Glow, the salon in the town square. "I don't see anything odd about it."

"At least there aren't too many with the right date," Sophie remarked. "We should be able to narrow down the suspects with this."

"I thought we'd be able to narrow down the suspects with the minutes of the town council meeting," I said, "but look how that turned out."

"Good point," Sophie replied.

"Here's poor Josef's will," Begonia said. "Wasn't that a wonderful funeral?"

"It was nothing like I expected," I said. "He seemed like a fascinating man. I wish I'd had the chance to meet him."

Begonia giggled. "Who knows with you? Maybe you will."

"That's funny," I said. "Hey, here's the deed to his house." I pulled the document from the pile and began to read.

"I'm sure he left the house to Felix," Millie said. "That's his only child."

"He did," I said, still reading. Everything looked in order.

"Spell's Bells. You'll never guess what I have here," Sophie said.

"Please say it's the smoking gun," I said.

"I don't know what that is, but this is a marriage license for Elsa Knightsbridge and Jasper Jansen," Sophie said.

"They're married?" I queried, peering over her shoulder at the document.

"No, this is the preliminary paperwork," Sophie said. "You get the marriage license filed beforehand, so they must be engaged." She frowned at me. "I'm surprised we haven't heard about this."

With the rumor mill in this town running at full tilt? Me too.

"We cleared Elsa," I said. "She seemed pretty annoyed about the whole thing. If anything, her mother's current state has caused her more harm than good."

"And her mother might know about the engagement, but they've decided to keep it quiet," Begonia said. "You know Mayor Knightsbridge, always politically maneuvering."

I pushed thoughts of Elsa and her impending marriage aside and we continued to review every document registered on that date. Nothing seemed out of the ordinary or suspicious.

"Well, this is another dead end," Millie complained.

My shoulders slumped. I was certain we'd find what we needed here. "Let's refile these papers and tell Astrid to lock up."

Lucy came flying out of the entrance to the Mayor's

Mansion, a frantic expression on her face. "Thank the stars that you're here."

"Why?" I asked. "What's going on?"

"The mayor showed up at the office today. Apparently, she stole the babysitter's wand and did a spell that cemented her feet to the floor. Then she marched in here and started giving orders."

"What kind of orders?" Was she actually trying to perform her duties as mayor?

"Come and see for yourself," Lucy said.

I followed her sparkling pink wings into the mayor's office. There were six of her employees seated on the floor in a circle. Mayor Knightsbridge fluttered around them, pointing at each one with her wand as she went. "Duck, duck, duck."

With each touch of her wand, the employee became the animal she named. Before long, the circle was filled with five ducks and one goose.

"Mayor Knightsbridge," Lucy scolded. "What did I tell you about playing games in the office?"

The mayor mimicked Lucy's tone.

"Mayor, do be a good girl and turn them back into… whatever they were." I wasn't sure which types of supernaturals the mayor employed.

The mayor crossed her arms and huffed. "Make me."

Uh oh.

Lucy and I exchanged worried glances. "She can be very stubborn at times," Lucy said.

"You don't say." We needed to consult with Elsa. She would have the best idea about how to handle her mother.

"Lucy, if you can get in touch with Elsa, I bet she will have some idea as to how to keep her mother in check."

"Elsa has been avoiding her mother as much as possible," Lucy said.

"Well, she's going to have to step up now," I said. "If we want to keep the situation contained until we can change them back, then we need her help."

"She's trying to issue a declaration that every Tuesday be Love a Unicorn Day," Lucy said.

"Well, at least that's positive," I said. I could imagine worse declarations.

"She may be a child, but she still has the mayor's intelligence. I tried to tell her that if she did as she was told I might take her to look at puppies and she totally called my bluff." Lucy threw up her hands. "I don't know what else to do. She's out of control."

"Lucy, you are every bit as capable of handling the town's affairs," I told her. "You know exactly how the mayor handles every situation. You've been watching her for years and assisting her. There is no one better equipped to handle this crisis than you."

Lucy's shoulder straightened and her wings stiffened. "You're absolutely right. Why am I doubting myself? I've been training for this moment since my first day on the job."

I clapped her on the shoulders. "Go get 'em, tiger."

She looked at me askance. "Emma, I'm a fairy, not a weretiger."

"Right." There wasn't time to explain every idiom in the human world.

I left Lucy in charge and decided to see how the other council members were faring. Outside of the mansion, I ran into Sophie and Begonia.

"Sedgwick told us you were here," Sophie said.

"He told you?" I looked up and saw him hovering overhead. "Oh, I see. Is there a problem?" What a ridiculous question. There seemed to be nothing but problems in Spellbound right now. I was racing from one fire to another and none of them was subsiding.

"It's Lady Weatherby," Begonia said. "She's demanding to see her mother."

That was an interesting development. "She wants to see Agnes?"

Begonia nodded. "The care home won't let her in, though. They said she's got to be accompanied by an adult."

I smacked my forehead. "Okay, I'll head

"I wouldn't want to miss the chance to see Lady Weatherby and Agnes together," Begonia said.

"Probably best if you don't. Agnes loves an audience. Who knows what she'll do?" I'd need to leave my wand in the car. The Spellbound Care Home had a strict policy on magical paraphernalia. I'd made the mistake of bringing my wand the first time I visited Agnes and chaos ensued. I'd never make that mistake again.

I stowed away my wand and headed over to the care home on foot since it wasn't far from the Mayor's Mansion.

I spotted Lady Weatherby in the lobby, sitting cross-legged in front of a coffee table with crayons and paper.

"That's a pretty picture," I said, crossing the room to peer over her shoulder. It was more than pretty—it was amazing. She may have had the mental state of a child, but she had the skills of a seasoned artist.

"It's my cat, Chairman Meow. Isn't he beautiful?"

The cat in the picture looked nothing like the tornado of midnight fluff. The drawing was much more elegant and mesmerizing. She even managed to do shading with the grey crayon.

"You should hang this on your refrigerator," I told her. "It's very good."

She flashed a proud smile. "I want to show my mom, but they won't let me in without a grown-up. Will you come in with me?"

"Yes, of course. Agnes and I are old friends."

Lady Weatherby rose to her feet and placed her hand in mine. It felt odd to have the head of the coven holding my hand, especially when her physical form still belonged to the adult version of J.R. Weatherby.

We approached the pixie at the reception desk.

"Miss Hart," she said brightly. "It's so good to see you again. It seems like only yesterday."

"That's because it was only a few days ago," I pointed out.

"I understand this young lady would like to visit with her mother," the pixie said. "As long as you stay with her, she's welcome to go inside."

Lady Weatherby jumped up and down with excitement. "I'm going to see my mommy."

I couldn't decide whether to laugh or cry. Lady Weatherby seemed so vulnerable. It was a striking contrast to her usual standoffish manner.

"Your mother may have company," I warned her. "Let me go in first and make sure that she's…" I almost said decent, but I didn't want to put any thoughts in Lady Weatherby's head. "I'll make sure she's not in the bath."

"My mother detests baths," Lady Weatherby said.

I couldn't even get a white lie past the child form of Lady Weatherby. Ugh. She was too sharp for me even as a seven-year-old.

We made our way down the corridor and I exchanged greetings with a few residents who recognized me from my volunteer work with Daniel.

Lady Weatherby gave me a quizzical look. "Everyone knows you here, Emma. That's so weird."

It was weird for me to hear Lady Weatherby call me Emma when the adult version only referred to me as Miss Hart.

Agnes was in the doorway when we arrived, chatting with a healer. Her eyes popped when she saw me approach with her daughter. Although I didn't know the particulars, I knew their relationship was a difficult one.

"Mommy," Lady Weatherby cried, and ran toward Agnes. She threw her arms around the old witch, nearly knocking her over. The healer wisely took that as her cue to leave.

"It's true then," Agnes said, more to me. "I heard about the spell, but I didn't quite believe it." She disentangled herself from her daughter. "What brings you here, Jacinda Ruth?"

"Did you know I'm head of the coven now?" Lady Weatherby asked, bubbling with excitement.

"Yes, yes. I know all about it. Don't you remember? I was there."

Agnes moved into her room and Lady Weatherby skipped behind her, her headdress falling askew in the process. She looked…adorable.

"I don't suppose you smuggled in any treats?" Agnes asked.

"No," I replied firmly. I wasn't going down that road again. I'd already puked once in her toilet. That was enough.

"I have treats," Lady Weatherby replied, and pulled several pieces of colorful candy from her cloak pocket.

"These look nice," Agnes said, accepting them.

"Do you like it in this place?" Lady Weatherby asked, twirling around so that her cloak billowed out like a bell.

"It's adequate," Agnes said.

"Do you resent me for not taking care of you?" Lady Weatherby asked. She began to fiddle with a few coins on the kitchenette counter.

"Resent is a big word for a little girl," Agnes said.

"I know lots of big words," Lady Weatherby said, lifting her chin. "I'm very smart."

Agnes reached up and patted her head, avoiding the twisted antlers of her headdress. "Yes, you are. You get that from your mother."

I felt like an intruder standing in the room with them. "Would you like me to wait outside?"

"No, you have to stay," Lady Weatherby insisted. "They said you have to accompany me, remember?"

"What's new and exciting in the coven, dear?" Agnes asked. "Why don't you sit down and tell me everything?"

Her demeanor fascinated me. This was a different Agnes to the wily and mischievous witch I'd come to know.

Instead of sitting in a chair, Lady Weatherby hopped up and down on the edge of the bed. "I guess you know about Emma here. She's not really one of ours, but we let her play with us."

I winced.

"Now, now, dear." Agnes mustered a smile. "We've accepted her, haven't we?"

Lady Weatherby giggled. "She's terrible at baking."

"Hey," I objected. "Cut me some slack. It's all new to me."

"Where are your friends, Mommy?" Lady Weatherby asked. "I'd like to meet them."

"Not today, pet," Agnes said. "Perhaps another time. I'd rather just talk to you. We haven't seen each other in quite some time."

Lady Weatherby beamed. "Do you want to play a game? You always have cards."

"That I do."

Agnes produced a deck of cards from her pocket and began to shuffle them. "Would you care to join us?"

"No, thank you," I said. "I'm going to sneak down the hall and see if Estella is around." Estella was a dwarf I'd met here when I'd come to see Agnes. "I'll make sure no one sees me."

I wandered around the care home for half an hour, talking to various residents, until Agnes found me in Estella's room.

"She's ready to go," Agnes said. "She says she's hungry and sleepy."

"I'll bet," I said. "It's been a busy day."

Back in her mother's room, Lady Weatherby bent forward and Agnes gently kissed her forehead.

"Take good care, pet," Agnes said. "You'll come to see me again soon, won't you?"

"Of course," Lady Weatherby replied. "You're my mother. I miss you."

Agnes tried to disguise her shock. "I miss you, too."

"We should go," I said, taking Lady Weatherby's hand. "We need to get you something to eat."

Her hand touched her stomach. "I would like a leg of lamb, if you don't mind."

Okay, I was expecting her to say 'ice cream' but whatever. "Sure. Let's find you a leg of lamb."

"That was always her favorite," Agnes said. "With a sprinkle of rosemary." She paused. "Do you think she'll be back to see me, once the spell is reversed?" There was a hint of wistfulness in her voice.

"I hope so," I said. "But you know your daughter better than anyone. She has a mind of her own."

"And where do you think she gets it?" Agnes said proudly.

I smiled. "Have a good day, Agnes. Try to stay out of trouble."

She leaned against the doorframe for support. "Terrible advice, Hart. Where's the fun in that?"

CHAPTER 13

In the midst of all of the chaos, I'd forgotten that I'd agreed to host the vampire séance for Gareth and his friends. I wasn't sure about hosting at my house, but I knew that it was the only appropriate place for them to reunite since my office was too small and the library was too public.

Kassandra was the first to arrive. She was nothing like I expected. Her dark hair was streaked with blonde and she sported a tongue ring. A punk psychic.

"You must be Kassandra," I said. "Please come in. I'm Emma."

Kassandra stepped into the foyer and glanced around. "Such interesting vibes I'm getting. What a great house with old bones."

"Thank you," I replied, although I wasn't certain that I could take credit for the great vibes since I'd only moved in a few months ago.

"Why is Gareth hiding downstairs?" Kassandra asked.

I laughed. "You can tell where he is? He's sulking. He wanted to be able to change his outfit for the reunion, but he hasn't figured out how to do that yet."

Kassandra smiled. "The life of a new ghost. Some things never change."

"Should I get him?"

Kassandra waved me off. "Let him sulk. We don't need him yet. Why don't you show me where I'll be performing?"

Performing was an interesting choice of words since, by all accounts, she was an actual psychic.

I showed her to the living room with its huge mantel and fireplace. She clapped her hands together and spun around.

"What a fabulous room." She walked over and pressed her open palms against the wall. "Oh, if these walls could talk."

"They'd tell you that your outfit is hideous," Gareth said. I turned to see him floating in the doorway, giving Kassandra the stink eye.

Kassandra inclined her head. "He's here now, isn't he?"

"You can't just see and hear him like I can?" I asked. I didn't know why, but I expected Kassandra to be able to communicate with him in exactly the same way I did.

She shook her head. "It doesn't work like that for me. I need a focal point. Almost like a physical vessel to bring him through."

I suppose that explained her use of the word performance. Her method required effort.

"I don't like her hair," Gareth said, folding his arms like a disgruntled toddler. "Hair doesn't need statement streaks."

"You don't like anyone's hair," I shot back. In fact, one of Gareth's favorite pastimes was criticizing the various states of my hair.

"I'd like to sit at the head of this table, if that's okay with you," Kassandra said. The long table previously resided in the dining room until my first poker night. After that, Gareth and I decided it was best to leave it in the living room for hosting purposes.

"Anything you want," I said. "The séance is for Gareth and his friends. I'm simply the hostess."

Kassandra placed a hand on my shoulder. "You're a good friend to him. Not everyone would be so welcoming."

I laughed. "I didn't exactly have a choice. He lived here first."

"They're here," Gareth called. He disappeared from view, probably going to critique their outfits before they walked through the door. Typical Gareth.

I followed him to the front door and, sure enough, five vampires stood on my front porch. Demetrius, Samson, Edgar, Dante, and Killian. Each was handsome in his own way, but Demetrius was the cream of the vampire crop. I stepped aside to let them pass.

"Come in," I said. "Gareth is excited to see you all again."

"And probably to talk our ears off about everything we've been doing wrong since his death," Samson said, prompting laughter from the others.

"No fair," Gareth complained. "They can't start taking the piss until Kassandra has worked her magic."

"Let's get started, shall we?" I said, guiding them into the living room. Kassandra sat at the head of the table, her hands clasped together.

"I'll need something of Gareth's," she said. "Preferably something of sentimental value."

Edgar chuckled. "Good luck finding that."

"Hey," Gareth said. "I can be sentimental."

At that moment, Magpie breezed into the room. Surprisingly, he didn't seem remotely bothered by the crowd. Several vampires backed away slightly at the sight of him.

"Devil in darkness," Edgar said. "You haven't gotten rid of that beast yet?"

Magpie seemed to know that he was the center of the

conversation. He jumped up onto the table and plopped down in the middle of it, licking his paws.

"He'll do," Kassandra said, and reached forward. Magpie seemed as surprised as anyone when she wrapped her arms around his hairless body and pulled him onto her lap.

"She can't…" Gareth began, but my look shut him up.

"Let her do what she needs to do," I told him.

"Everyone take a seat," Kassandra said. "This cat is vibrating with energy. He'll be a perfect conduit."

"A perfect conduit for evil," Samson muttered.

"Kettle meet pot," I said pointedly.

Samson fell silent.

Kassandra inhaled deeply and closed her eyes, stroking Magpie as she began to hum. I waited with baited breath for Magpie to sink his teeth into her arm, but he sat perfectly still, as though he sat on a woman's lap every day. Man, he was so annoying.

"I call you forth, Gareth," Kassandra said. "I call you forth to greet those who love you."

Gareth floated in the doorway. "I'm right here. She knows I'm right here, doesn't she?"

I shrugged. This was my first séance. What did I know?

Kassandra continued to hum until, without warning, she yanked one of Magpie's few hairs from his body and threw it into the fire behind her. Magpie yowled in protest and tried to jump from her lap, but she held firm.

"What is that crackpot doing to my cat?" Gareth demanded. "It's torture."

Kassandra's eyes flew open and she focused on him. "That crackpot is making you visible for you and your friends."

Gareth nearly fell backward.

"Gareth?" Edgar squinted. "Great damnation, it is you."

Samson looked to Kassandra. "Can we touch him?"

"Now that sounds promising," Gareth quipped.

Kassandra pursed her lips. "He's not really solid, but for a short while, you'll be able to see and hear each other. I urge you to make the most of it."

Magpie remained calm. Although I wasn't certain, I thought I even heard the soft sound of purring.

As Gareth floated over to the table for closer inspection, Demetrius broke into a broad grin. "You look fantastic for a ghost. The true death agrees with you."

"And you look great as always, you lucky bastard," Gareth said with a toothy smile.

"So the other times I've been here..." Demetrius began. "Were you here then?"

I knew what Demetrius was referring to. He'd visited me on several occasions, including two kisses on the front porch.

"No worries, Dem," Gareth said. "Your game is as good as ever."

The other vampires chuckled.

"On that note," Gareth said, "there's something I need to get off my chest before we lose our connection."

Oh wow. I didn't expect Gareth to use the séance for this reason, but I suppose it made sense.

"What is it?" Edgar asked. "Do you want us to deliver a message to Alison?" Alison had been Gareth's former fiancée. They'd broken off the engagement about a year before his death, though.

"No, Emma has spoken to Alison on my behalf." Gareth cleared his throat. "I wasn't honest with all of you in the years we've known each other. In truth, I wasn't honest with myself. It was silly of me, living so many years with a secret."

"What secret?" Edgar prodded gently.

"It's time I came out of the coffin," Gareth said. "Gentlemen, you're in the presence of a gay vampire."

I watched the reactions of the group, especially the Scripture-spouting Dante. I hoped for Gareth's sake that everyone was accepting.

Demetrius was the first one to speak. "Well, that explains the leather pants you used to own."

"And the disco ball," Edgar added.

"Ahem. I took ownership of the disco ball," Samson said.

"Anything you care to tell us then, Samson?" Gareth asked, and everyone laughed again.

"I like the way the light reflects off of it," Samson said. "It's very atmospheric."

"So I have an important question," Demetrius said, his dark eyes solemn. "Which one of us has the best butt?"

Gareth smiled "That's an easy one. You know it's you, Dem."

The chorus of laughter was music to my ears. Gareth's big secret was finally out and I felt elated for him. I was grateful that I could help give him this chance to share that important piece of himself he'd kept hidden.

"You have an owl on your porch," Demetrius said, peering out the window.

"No, Sedgwick is upstairs," I replied.

Demetrius suppressed a smile. "It's not your owl. This one doesn't look like he's cursing me under his breath."

I opened the window and the owl deposited a note into my hand.

"I recognize the owl," Killian said. "He belongs to Markos."

I felt everyone's eyes on me as I unrolled the message. It was a party invitation, to be held at the minotaur's house.

"Care to share with the class?" Gareth prodded.

"He's hosting a party," I said. "That's all."

Gareth performed his version of a happy dance, floating around the room and wiggling his hips. "You're in for a real treat. Markos's parties are legendary."

"So does everyone get invited?" I asked.

Edgar laughed. "Hardly. He likes to keep the odds in his favor, if you know what I mean."

"Not that the guy needs any help," Killian added. "Lucky bastard is a magnet for women."

I gave Killian a sympathetic smile. I'd first met him at Pandora's matchmaking office. He was a nice vampire struggling to find the right girl and settle down. Tale as old as time.

"If you're invited, it's because he's interested," Demetrius said, a bit disgruntled.

"You can't know that for certain," Samson said.

Demetrius met his gaze. "Yes, I do…because it's exactly what I would do."

I tucked the invitation in my pocket, feeling awkward. "Well, I don't know that I have time for a party anyway. I'm pretty busy with the council's problem and Russ's case."

Gareth crossed the room to stand beside me. "Take it from me, Emma. You only get one shot at life…" He hesitated. "Fine, some of us get two shots, but the point remains. Don't use work as an excuse not to live your life. Trust me on that one."

He whirled around and faced his guests. "So I want to hear all of the latest gossip from the golf course. Has anyone's handicap improved? I don't know how much longer we'll be able to see each other." He glanced at Kassandra, who shrugged.

"It's always a crapshoot," she said, stroking Magpie. She reminded me of the quintessential evil mastermind, sitting in the armchair with a hairless cat.

I slipped out of the room and pulled out the invitation to read it again. Markos seemed like a good guy and everyone liked him. Not to mention he didn't have the womanizing reputation of Daniel or Demetrius.

You should go, Princess Party Pooper, Sedgwick said, appearing on the banister.

"If I'm a party pooper, then why should I go?" I shot back. "Doesn't that mean I'll ruin it?"

You should go so that I get a night off, he replied. *It's a matter of complete self-interest.*

"You're the worst," I said.

"Emma?"

I spun around. "Hey, Dem. Do you need something?"

"Just wanted to make sure you haven't been experiencing any of the lawlessness around here that other residents have."

"No," I said. "My yard seems to have been spared from the parade of shifting shifters."

He grinned and I saw the hint of his fangs. "Good to hear."

As I turned to go upstairs, a thought occurred to me. "Demetrius, are you the one who warded my property?"

His brow lifted. "Am I the one who…No, I did not ward your property."

Something in his expression suggested he was lying, so I tried again. "Demetrius, did you have someone else ward my property?"

He lowered his gaze, his usual swagger nowhere to be seen. "I may have asked a friend to do a protective spell." His eyes met mine. "I hope you're not upset."

I held the banister to steady myself. Demetrius had the property warded to protect me, not Daniel. The vampire was more thoughtful than I gave him credit for.

"Thank you, Demetrius. I'm not upset. It was very kind of you to think of me."

"I know you're capable of taking care of yourself," he said. "I hope you don't take it the wrong way."

My heart softened. "Not at all. It's nice that you care."

"I do," he said, his dark eyes earnest. "I should get back to the others. I don't want to miss too much of Gareth."

"No, you really don't. Goodnight, Dem."

"Goodnight, Emma."

I climbed the steps to my bedroom. From the comfort of my bed, I listened to the raucous sounds of the séance until I fell fast asleep.

CHAPTER 14

I AWOKE to the unpleasant sound of Sedgwick screeching. I bolted upright in bed and ripped off my eye mask.

"What's wrong?" I glanced wildly around the room, my heart pounding.

You're going to be late for school, he said.

I looked at the clock on my bedside table. Class was due to start in ten minutes.

"What happened?" I demanded, throwing back the covers and running into the bathroom. I was almost never late. To me, punctuality was a sign of respect for the other person. "Why did I oversleep?"

I don't know, Sedgwick said. *You seemed dead to the world.*

"Where's Gareth?" He was normally eager to tick off the squandered seconds in my ear.

I haven't seen him this morning.

It wasn't a complete surprise. Gareth had been practicing trying to pop up in more places around town. He was probably doing his ghostly best to haunt the disco.

Not at this early hour, Sedgwick said. *The disco would be midnight at the earliest.*

"Stop eavesdropping on my thoughts," I shouted, as I shoved a toothbrush in my mouth. There was no time for food, so I focused on eradicating my morning breath. Nobody deserved to inhale those fumes.

As I brushed my hair, I realized something was wrong. Very wrong.

"Sedgwick?"

I am not going to critique your hair. That's Gareth's job.

"Not that. Can you see me in the mirror?"

He flapped his wings behind me. *Now that's interesting.*

I waved my arms but saw nothing reflected in the glass. I lifted the toothbrush again and watched the reflection as it floated in the air.

"But you can see me, right?" I asked.

Unfortunately.

What on earth was happening? "Why am I invisible?"

You have been eating less lately.

"Ha ha. What am I supposed to do? I can't go to class if I'm invisible."

You have to do something.

"Do you think they'll be able to hear me even if they can't see me?"

Only one way to find out.

I dressed quickly and hurried out of the house.

Meet you there, I told Sedgwick.

I saw a few gobsmacked looks as the seemingly driverless Volvo rolled into town. After a few more shocked faces, I began to laugh. It occurred to me that being invisible might be fun.

By the time I arrived in class, Professor Holmes was mid-lecture. He stopped when the door blew open. "Sophie, would you mind closing the door? I'm not sure where that gust of wind came from."

I closed the door before Sophie reached it.

"Look, there's Sedgwick," Laurel said. "But where's Emma?"

"I'm right here," I said.

"That's odd," Sophie said. "Sedgwick wouldn't come without her."

"He didn't," I shouted.

"Sometimes he gets here first if she walks," Begonia pointed out.

Professor Holmes rustled the papers on his desk. "Witches, let's get back to the lesson. We'll welcome Emma whenever she chooses to appear."

"I choose to appear right now," I said, but no dice.

You may as well take advantage of the situation, Sedgwick said. *Go back to bed*.

I can write a note, I said. I ran past the other girls to the teacher's desk. I took a quill and began to scribble on the nearest piece of parchment.

"Professor," Millie cried. "Your quill is moving."

The look on the elderly wizard's face was priceless.

What are you writing? Sedgwick asked.

"I am invisible," Professor Holmes read aloud. "P.S. It's Emma." He stared at the spot where I stood. "You're invisible?"

"Apparently."

I continued to write and he watched in anticipation as each word formed on the page. "She doesn't know what happened," he told the class. "She woke up like this."

"What fun!" Begonia said.

"Were you trying to do a spell at home?" Sophie asked.

"No," Professor Holmes said, reading my answer. He stroked his chin. "Which means someone did this to you."

"Why would anyone want her invisible?" Laurel asked.

"She's been following up on leads, trying to figure out

who put the spell on Stan and the town council," Begonia said. "Maybe she got too close to the truth."

"Good thinking, Begonia," Professor Holmes said. "We'll need to retrace your steps. Make a list of everyone you've spoken with in the last few days and we'll start with that."

The last few days? Between Russ and the town council, that was a ridiculously long list.

"But what if it's not related to the youth spell?" Sophie asked. "Then we're wasting valuable time talking to irrelevant people."

"That happens to me all the time," Millie said.

Begonia frowned. "You sound like Jemima."

"I was kidding," Millie said sheepishly, but we all knew better.

Professor Holmes placed a fresh sheet of parchment on the desk. "Here you go, Emma. Don't spare us the details."

I wrote down as many names as I could remember. It didn't help that I'd been all around town the past couple of days. Anyone I passed could have done this to me.

"Tell us everywhere you ate and drank too," Millie added. "It could have been a potion."

Professor Holmes beamed. "My students are making me proud today."

"Just today?" Millie pouted.

Professor Holmes swatted the air. "For nature's sake, Millie. Stop fishing for compliments."

Millie's cheeks burned crimson.

My hand was beginning to cramp from all the writing. I couldn't remember the last time I'd handwritten so much at once. I felt a pang of longing for my laptop.

"All done," I announced, not that anyone could hear me.

Professor Holmes noticed when the quill returned to its usual place. "She must be finished." He scanned the information before addressing the group. "I suggest we split up to save time."

"What about today's lesson?" Millie asked, always the eager star pupil.

"Today's lesson is how to help a friend in need," Professor Holmes said. "I trust you are interested to learn more about that."

"Of course," Millie said, straightening her shoulders. "Just tell me where to start."

"What about you?" Professor Holmes asked me. "What will you do?" He gave me a dismissive wave. "On second thought, don't tell me. It might be best if you slink around town and eavesdrop. Perhaps you'll learn something useful."

Not a bad idea.

Or maybe it is, Sedgwick said. *Sometimes you learn things you'd rather not know.*

True, but what choice do I have? I'll meet you outside Brew-Ha-Ha. If there's gossip happening, that's a good place to start.

You just want to steal a sip of someone's latte, Sedgwick said.

I laughed. My familiar knew me too well.

Brew-Ha-Ha was packed at this hour. The morning rush seemed to last until lunchtime. I slipped in behind two fairies and moved clockwise around the room.

People always talk about wanting to be a fly on the wall, but I never really understood the desire until now. Even though it was wrong to eavesdrop on private conversations, I found myself enjoying the experience. No one saw me. No one paid attention to me. Sadly, it was likely a glimpse into my future—when I became a woman of a certain age.

Most of the conversations I overheard were banal. Complaints about family members. Job interview. Fears about money. These were conversations I could have heard in my local Starbucks. The only difference was that some of the patrons sported wings or pointy ears.

Across the room, I spotted the three youngest harpies. Darcy, Calliope, and Freya Minor were chowing down on scones and sipping tea. Darcy had a hand in every philanthropic pot in town. She probably came a close second to Myra, the church administrator, in terms of access to gossip. A good place to start then.

"She accused me of not cleaning the sink thoroughly enough," Darcy grumbled. "Again. Like I don't have enough on my plate."

"I wish Grandmother would relent and let us hire a fairy cleaning service," Calliope said. "It would alleviate so many of these arguments."

"Not all of them," Freya said. "If she tells me one more time to pluck my eyebrows, I'm going to pluck her eyes out with my talons."

Calliope smiled. "Your eyebrows are perfect just the way they are."

"Thanks, sis." Freya relaxed and bit into her scone.

"I have something to confess," Calliope said, and my ears perked up. "I'm thinking about trying Pandora's matchmaking service."

"What?" her sisters cried in unison.

Calliope hid behind her enormous teacup. "We keep talking about how we don't meet any men, but we don't do anything about it."

"I meet men all the time," Darcy said primly. "They simply can't handle a strong woman."

"You're not strong. You're a relentless taskmaster," Freya said. "There's a difference."

Calliope placed a hand on her younger sister's arm. "Okay, let's not go there right now. Save the arguments for the privacy of our own home."

So Calliope's confession was that she wanted to use a matchmaker. Interesting, but not the kind of information I was seeking.

I turned and caught a glimpse of Myra placing an order at the counter. Jackpot! As the church administrator, the gnome had taken to hearing confessions in the Spellbound church. If anyone had confessed to the youth spell, she'd be the one to have heard it.

I hovered behind her, listening intently to her conversation with Henrik, the barista who'd been the object of Russ's wrath.

"I heard he threw a sledgehammer at you, and it crushed the side of Edgar's face," Myra said.

Henrik chuckled. "It was a beer bottle and Edgar is recovering nicely."

Ah, the inevitable outcome of whisper down the lane.

"I passed Mayor Knightsbridge and Juliet Montlake on my way here, jumping rope at the playground," Myra said, paying for her drink. "Any word on that disaster?"

Hmm. If Myra was hitting up the barista for gossip, that meant she didn't know anything.

Henrik shook his Mohawk. "I just wish Sheriff Hugo would sort it out. The town is a mess. I caught two elves trying to vandalize the windows last night with fairy paint. They ran when they saw me come outside with my spear."

I didn't think he needed a spear to make anyone run. The berserker looked intimidating enough without a weapon.

"It feels like no one's in charge," Myra said, shuddering. "I don't care for it."

Me neither. I left Myra and Henrik and was about to give up when I heard a reference to Josef, the recently deceased wizard.

"Did you go to the wake?" an unfamiliar elf asked. I moved closer to their table to listen.

"I went on the second day," the dwarf replied. Upon closer inspection, I realized it was Deacon, the owner of the jewelry store. His store had been robbed by a goblin called Mumford, the defendant in my very first case in Spellbound.

"I always try to attend on the first day before the smell sets in," the elf said.

"That's smart," Deacon said. "I had to work on the first day. Were there a lot of mourners?"

"I don't know about mourners, but there were certainly a lot of nosy residents walking around. His house is massive, isn't it?"

"Some of those rooms reminded me of a museum," Deacon said. "Did you check out the library on the second floor? He seemed to be hoarding old grimoires. I wonder if the coven knows about that."

The elf sipped his tea. "If they didn't before, they do now. I saw a dozen people up there, flipping through the books. There were some crazy spells in there. Did you read any of them?"

Deacon laughed, a rumbling sound that came straight from his stomach. "I saw one about how to obtain anything you want from the universe. Talk about vague and broad." He shook his head. "Sometimes I don't know what these witches and wizards are thinking."

"No kidding," the elf said. "I saw one spell about how to get a beach body in five minutes. Not much use around here."

"Well, there's always Swan Lake. We get a partial shoreline."

I'd heard enough. I hadn't attended the wake, but now I felt that I should go investigate the books in the wizard's library, assuming the books were still there. I'd have to drive Sigmund. From what I remembered, the house was too far to walk.

Sedgwick was perched on the roof of the car when I arrived.

Where are you going? Sedgwick asked.

"I'm taking a ride to a dead wizard's house," I said. "Do you want to come?"

Sedgwick tilted his head, debating. *What's in it for me?*

"What kind of question is that? You're my familiar. You're supposed to be more like me."

"Says who? Just because we can communicate doesn't mean we share a personality."

That seemed to be one way in which he was different from the witches' cat familiars. We really didn't share a similar personality.

"The house will be empty," I said. "There are sure to be mice running around."

Good enough for me, Sedgwick said.

I drove further away from downtown to where the houses were bigger and further apart. A long, dirt road led me to the wizard's estate. There was no sign of life, not that I expected there to be. This was not the time to discover I could see another ghost. Then again, maybe the wizard would have helpful information.

The front door was unlocked so I let myself in. Sedgwick flew in after me, immediately disappearing down a dark hallway. The house was bursting with interesting artifacts. He was clearly a collector, although I didn't know of what. There were crystals of various colors, shapes, and sizes. Each had its own pedestal. He clearly took care of them. There wasn't a speck of dust on any of the pieces and, with all of their jagged edges, these were prime dust magnets.

I headed upstairs to the second floor to find the library that Deacon and the elf had mentioned. It wasn't hard to find. There was a large bookcase to my right crammed with leather-bound books. In the middle of the room stood a table with a raised stand. Although the space was empty now, it looked like it had once supported a book. It was surprising that no one in the coven noticed the number of spell books in the house. Many witches and wizards had attended the wake. I'd need to ask Professor Holmes why they were unconcerned. It seemed unwise to leave such potent books out for public consumption. If witches weren't even permitted to have a grimoire until graduation from the academy, it seemed risky to leave books like these out for anyone to view or steal. I studied the empty space. What if there had been a grimoire here during the wake and someone had stolen it? Perhaps the missing grimoire contained the youth spell. If we found the book, then we would find the spell caster.

I looked around the room and sighed. Trying to find a missing book of spells in Spellbound was worse than a needle in a haystack. I didn't even know the title of the missing book or what it looked like, assuming I was right in the first place. I wondered if anyone had catalogued his estate after his death. Based on the state of the house, my guess was not yet.

Find anything good? Sedgwick flew in and perched on the stand.

"Do you think the wizard kept records of his belongings?" I asked. "Maybe his own personal card catalog for this library?"

What are you looking for?

"A missing grimoire, I think. It may have rested right where you are now. It's just a hunch, but I'd like to pursue it."

I didn't see any evidence of a catalogue or list of inventory in the library. I did a quick tour of the rest of the house but saw no evidence of the grimoire.

"Let's go," I told Sedgwick.

Home?

"You can go home," I said. "I'm going to the office to write a note for Althea. I need to tell her what's going on with me. I can't defend Russ if I'm invisible."

Suit yourself.

I left the contents of the house exactly as I found them and returned to my car. For a fleeting moment, I thought being invisible would be a welcome break from responsibility, but it seemed to translate into more work.

Just another lucky day for Emma Hart.

CHAPTER 15

I WAS SHOCKED to enter my office and see Gareth floating around the room.

"Here you are," I said. "Where have you been all morning? I'm having a crisis."

"Your hair can hardly be considered a crisis," he replied. "All you need to do is run a brush through it every now and again and ta da—the beast is tamed."

I groaned. "I am not talking about my hair."

"That's part of the problem," Gareth said, clucking his tongue. "Denial."

I slapped my forehead in frustration as the connecting door opened and Althea breezed in with the watering can.

"Tell her she's not giving the plant enough water," Gareth said.

"I can't," I said.

Althea strolled right past me and tipped the water into the plant.

Gareth whistled. "Talk about the cold shoulder. What did you do to annoy her? You insulted her snakes, didn't you? They're very sensitive reptiles."

Althea stopped and looked around the room. "Are you in here, Gareth? I feel a feminine presence, so I know it isn't Emma."

Gareth howled with laughter. "Excellent. She's really gunning for you today."

"She's not," I said. "She can't see me."

"Nice try," he said.

I jumped in front of Althea and waved my hands in front of her face. She barely blinked. Instead, she returned to her office and closed the door.

I faced Gareth, hands on hips. "Believe me now?"

His jaw dropped. "What happened to you? Great damnation, are you dead?" His pale face drained of any remaining color. "Oh no. Poor Magpie."

"You think I'm dead and your cat is the one you feel sorry for?" I asked in disbelief. "Thankfully, I'm not dead. Just invisible."

He circled me. "Can Sedgwick see you?"

"Yes, but no one else seems able to hear me or see me."

"Lucky them."

"Yes, you and Sedgwick are on the same page with that one." I sat at my desk and composed a note to Althea. "I need to figure out who did this to me and how to turn visible again. The remedial witches and Professor Holmes are looking into it."

"So what will you do?"

"Eavesdropping seems to be my best bet. I've picked up a few nuggets already. Now I'm going to head over to the sheriff's office and see what progress he's made."

Gareth sighed dramatically. "Oh, I'm so jealous. Haunting the sheriff would be a dream come true."

"Have you tried to materialize over there?"

"No, I didn't spend a significant amount of time there. It seems I need a closer connection to a place." He gave me a naughty grin. "You should drop in on Daniel while you're out of sight."

I gasped. "Never. Why would I do such a thing?"

"Why wouldn't you?"

"And what do you think that will achieve? You think he'll happen to be talking to himself about me when I'm there?"

He shrugged. "Worth a try. Maybe scribble your name in the foggy bathroom mirror with a heart around it and see how he reacts."

"That's creepy."

He warmed to the suggestion. "Aye, it is. Please do that and report back."

"I'll do no such thing. Besides, I don't think I want to know what Daniel says about me when I'm not around. What if it isn't what I hope?"

"Then at least you know," he said, more softly now. "Then you can accept it and move on."

I hated when Gareth made sense. "I'll think about it. I have more important matters to attend to right now," I said, and headed for the door.

"I expect a full briefing this evening," he called after me.

"Dream on, vampire ghost."

I waited a good fifteen minutes for the door to the sheriff's office to open before I could slip inside. Too bad I wasn't a ghost, then I wouldn't need an open door.

Astrid was standing at the desk, engaged in conversation with the centaur. Her tense expression contrasted sharply with the sheriff's bored one.

"We need to get to the bottom of the spell," Astrid said. "The town council can't stay like this forever. It's causing too many problems. Some young werewolf ripped up a parking ticket in front of me this morning."

"The coven doesn't seem able to reverse it," Sheriff Hugo replied. "Lady Weatherby is our best chance and she's too busy playing with dolls to do anything."

"What about one of the older witches?" Astrid asked. "Have you considered asking Agnes?"

Sheriff Hugo's dark eyes glinted. "I do not need the help of that senile old witch."

"You need help, though," Astrid said. "You admit that much, right?"

"Tread carefully, Astrid," he said. A warning tone.

The Valkyrie threw up her hands in frustration. "Lord Gilder apparently showed up at the blood bank and demanded his share like a spoiled brat. Mayor Knightsbridge wants the outside of her mansion painted hot pink. With sparkles. Things are only going to get worse if we don't do something."

The sheriff grabbed his wallet from the desk and shoved it in his back pocket. "Fine. I'll ask around at the country club."

Astrid gaped in disbelief. "Are you seriously going to the club now?"

"My tee time was already scheduled. The club has a twenty-four hour cancellation policy."

"And this crisis has been going on longer than twenty-four hours."

"I thought the spell would only last a day," he argued. "That it would wear off by itself. I didn't realize it was one that had to be reversed."

Astrid's voice softened. "Sheriff, the mayor is your friend. She'd want you to be doing everything in your power to help her."

"I am helping her," he said. "Do you know how many power brokers in this town hang out at the country club? Someone there will have information."

Astrid's jaw stiffened. "Tell me, sir. How many solid leads have you ever gotten on the golf course?"

The centaur pointed a finger at her. "Remember your place. You're *my* deputy, not the other way around."

"Yes, sir." Astrid watched as he left the office. The second the door clicked behind him, she mumbled, "Jackass."

I suspected he was lazy and incompetent, but this moment proved it.

"Oh, Astrid," I said, sighing deeply. "You really have your work cut out for you."

As much as I knew it was wrong to follow Daniel when he didn't know I was there, I couldn't help myself. I blamed Gareth for planting the seed in my mind. He was right, though. I had a rare opportunity to observe him and I didn't want to waste it. It was unlikely I'd ever get a chance like this again.

I was relieved when he walked northeast, past the library and the Mayor's Mansion. If he'd flown, there would have been no way for me to follow inconspicuously. I had no interest in getting on a broomstick when I was visible, let alone invisible. I had to admit, it was fun to watch him. I loved the way he admired the façade of the candle shop as he walked by and how he whistled back to a bird that had made a nest on top of a nearby fey lantern. He may not have been in tune with my feelings, but he certainly was in tune with his environment. He loved this town. That much was clear. For all of his tragic misery—and I certainly understood his depression—he harbored a love for this place greater than he probably knew.

He finally made his way to a sweet Craftsman-style home about three blocks north of the Mayor's Mansion. As he hopped up the front porch steps, I stood behind a nearby tree. I wasn't sure why I was hiding since no one could see me. Stupid instinct.

The front door opened to reveal Elsa Knightsbridge. I sucked in a breath. Was he taking my advice? Was he finally going to apologize in person?

I hurried to the front porch to hear what he was going to say. Although I felt guilty about it, I figured I could offer constructive criticism in the event that it didn't go as planned. If he was going to be making apologies to dozens of women in Spellbound, he might need a few pointers.

"What are you doing here?" she demanded. Her full red lips formed a straight line. Even without her bitter tone, her body language said it all. Her lean frame still managed to fill the doorway, blocking any possible passage by Daniel.

"I'm here to talk to you, if that's okay," he said. "There are a few things I'd like to say that are long overdue."

She crossed her arms and glared at him. "Jasper isn't here. He won't like it if he learns that I spoke to you alone." Her eyes glittered like stones. Daniel had more groveling to do.

"Listen. You have every right not to let me speak," he said. "To be perfectly honest, this apology is for my benefit. I only hope it helps you too."

Did he really think it was selfish to apologize? I didn't see it that way at all. To my complete surprise, she relented.

"Come in, but be quick," she said. "I don't need tongues wagging. We all know how the gossip mill operates around here."

He crossed the threshold and I hurried in right behind him. The interior was as cool and stylish as Elsa herself. Sparkling silver walls and metal objets d'art were everywhere I turned. It didn't match the exterior of the house at all, yet somehow it worked.

Elsa fluttered toward the kitchen. "Can I offer you anything? Do you still like gossamer tea?"

He gave her a small smile. "You remember."

"How could I forget? I had dozens of canisters of it left over after you dumped me." Her expression clouded over, remembering.

"Technically, I didn't dump you. You dumped me."

She whirled around, her eyes flashing angrily. "Only because you cheated on me. You forced my hand. What did you expect me to do?"

"Forgive me," he said quietly. "I expected you to forgive me. And that was wrong. And what I did to you was wrong."

Although she busied herself in the kitchen, I could tell she was listening intently. Her hand shook slightly as she took a mug from the cupboard and set it on the counter. There was no need to boil a kettle. She simply poured water from a jug into the mug and tapped it with her finger. Voilà. Boiled water. She sprinkled in what I assumed was gossamer tea and let it steep.

"And it's only taken you how long to admit this?" she said finally.

"Better late than never, right?"

"What on earth has prompted this transformation?" She tapped her elegant fingernails against her chin. "Oh yes, let me hazard a guess. That sweet little witch you've been hanging around with. What's her name? Gemma?"

He stood across from her at the counter. I was surprised to see him grinning. "Her name is Emma and you know it." He shook his head. "Same old jealous Elsa."

Elsa bristled. "Jealous? Why should I be jealous of someone with such bad luck in life and such poor choice in friends?" She gave him a pointed look.

"I'm here to ask your forgiveness," he said. "Obviously, you're under no obligation to give it, but that's the reason I'm here. I hope you'll consider it. I know we parted on bad terms, but I know your heart, Elsa, and it's a good one."

She handed him the mug. "You are as handsome and charming as ever, Daniel Starr. However do you manage it?"

"And I bet you still make the best gossamer tea in town." He took a tentative sip of the tea. "Yep. Still do. I'm glad that hasn't changed."

Elsa tilted her head. "Jasper and I are engaged. It's a big secret."

"Why a secret?" Daniel asked. "I can't imagine Jasper is ashamed of marrying the most beautiful fairy in all of Spellbound."

A blush crept into her chiseled cheekbones. "Mother isn't a fan of his family, you see."

"Your mother isn't a fan of anyone except her reflection in the mirror."

Elsa laughed. "Oh, Daniel. You know us so well."

A chill sliced through my veins. What was happening here? Were they…flirting? He was supposed to be here to apologize. To turn over a new leaf, not to retread old ground.

"It is difficult for Jasper, I admit," she said, coming around to Daniel's side of the counter. "You are such a hard act to follow, after all."

He took another sip of tea and peered down at her. "Am I? I seem to recall you wishing me dead a thousand different ways. Surely Jasper has done better than that."

She smiled up at him. "He is very sweet and he dotes on me. Rather like you once did." She ran a hand down his arm and a knot formed in my stomach. "I think I chose him because he reminded me of you, except without the misery."

"Only a fool would betray you," he said.

She laughed, lightly this time. "You were always willing to admit your shortcomings. It just didn't stop you from having them."

I really didn't like the way he looked at her now. It was the way I wanted him to look at me. The way he looked at me at the Spellbound High School prom after we'd kissed. A fleeting look, but one I'd never forget.

"Do you think your mother will ever forgive me?" he asked. "I suppose she should be next on my list."

Elsa shook her head. "Poor Mother. Perhaps you should apologize now while she's in her toddler state. She might be more likely to forgive you. Or kick you in the shins and run away."

"I hear you've been helping out while she's been…incapacitated."

Elsa nodded. "Lucy has as well. It takes a village, as you well know. This whole thing has reminded me how thankless Mother's job is. The woman is a saint."

Daniel chuckled. "I do believe that is the nicest thing I've ever heard you say about her."

"Seeing her like this has reminded me of my own behavior. I see what she's had to deal with all these years. I can't have been an easy fairy to raise." She lowered her gaze. "Nor an easy fairy to love."

Daniel set down his mug and placed his hands on her shoulders. "Elsa Knightsbridge, I am here to apologize to you. Don't you dare apologize to me. You're not to blame for what happened."

Her gaze traveled to his hand on her shoulder. "But I am to blame, Daniel. I was controlling and needy. I pushed you away. I didn't trust you because of your history."

"And with good reason," he exclaimed. "I deserved every bit of your mistrust. And I proved exactly why."

She reached up and curled her fingers around his. Nausea rolled over me.

"Have you thought about me since our breakup?" she asked. "Because I have thought a lot about you. To be honest, I still think about you now."

"What about Jasper?" he asked.

She inched closer to him. "I told you. He's nothing more than a lesser version of you. He will never be the man that you are. It's called settling. Perhaps you've heard of it."

Daniel gazed into her eyes. "But I'm not a man at all, remember? I'm an angel, and a fallen one at that. You should hold on to Jasper. I'm sure he's a better match for you."

She slid her hands down his chest and my pulse quickened. This was not going at all the way I thought it would.

"Tell me, Daniel. Do you feel anything for me? Have you missed me at all?"

He covered her hands with his. "I've thought often about those I've wronged, you first and foremost. You were, after all, my last and final relationship."

Elsa allowed herself a tiny smile. "So no one has managed to follow in my esteemed footsteps then?"

Me, I wanted to shout. *I am the next phase of his life*. Even if I had shouted, they wouldn't have heard me. Nor would it have mattered. I couldn't control Daniel any more then Elsa could. He didn't love me. He was my friend and the sooner I accepted that fact, the easier it would be for me to move on.

I couldn't stay and watch another second of the happy reunion. I knew what was coming next and I didn't want the image burned in my brain for eternity. It was my own fault for sneaking around. I deserved what I'd seen.

I returned to the front door and opened it as quietly as I could. They were so engrossed in each other, I knew they wouldn't hear the gentle click of the door as it closed behind me. It was a long walk home, and I cried every step of the way. The good thing about being invisible was that no one noticed.

CHAPTER 16

I LEFT ELSA'S HOUSE, not sure where to go next. My head was spinning and I couldn't quite grasp what I'd just witnessed. Maybe this was all a bad dream. Maybe I was like Freddie, the dwarf trapped in an enchanted sleep. Instead of pleasant dreams, though, I was in a walking nightmare.

Tears blinded me and I bumped into passersby left and right, but they only saw empty air. I didn't want to go home. Gareth would want to know what was wrong and I couldn't talk about it. Up ahead, the church spire loomed above all of the other buildings. It hypnotized me, drawing me to it. Although I wasn't a religious person, I found the gorgeous church to be a soothing refuge. I attended heart therapy in the basement, but I loved everything about the church—its stained-glass windows, statues, and intricate woodwork.

The door was open when I arrived so I took it as a sign. I walked down the aisle to the first pew and sat. Was I supposed to kneel? There was a little running board in front of my feet and I wasn't sure whether to use it for my feet or my knees.

I needed to clear my head. Although I felt betrayed by

Daniel, I knew that wasn't fair. He never promised me anything more than friendship. True, he told me he would swear off the opposite sex and devote himself to philanthropy, but if Elsa was his true love, then maybe she would be the one to lead him to redemption. Just because she was a spoiled brat didn't mean she wasn't capable of kindness and compassion, right?

I only enjoyed the quiet for a few minutes. I heard footsteps and turned around to see Dante enter. Instinctively, I ducked behind the pew, forgetting my invisibility once again. To my dismay, he took the seat behind me. I remained sprawled across the pew, debating whether to leave. It really shouldn't have been a surprise that the Scripture-spouting vampire attended church.

"God grant me the serenity to accept the things I cannot change," Dante said, and I recognized the beginning of the Serenity Prayer. My college roommate had a plaque on her desk bearing the quote. "Courage to change the things I can and the wisdom to know the difference."

I remembered Gareth's petition to have holy water removed from the church. He must have been thinking of vampires like Dante when he'd drafted it.

"God forgive me for the following," Dante began. "Number one. I used Samson's toothbrush without his knowledge after eating a garlic and onion bagel. I couldn't find mine and I know that's no excuse, but I really needed to brush my teeth because you know what garlic does to my breath. I should have confessed to him when he noticed his toothbrush was two inches further to the right than normal, but I blamed the cleaning service for moving it."

I hoped Myra was taking notes because if he was leading off with this one, I had the feeling he had a lot of minor confessions to get through.

"Number two. I went to sleep last night without saying

my prayers. I was tired and enjoyed one too many cocktails. Number three. I was envious of my friends. Demetrius because I covet his good looks and the ease with which he attracts women. And Gareth…"

My ears perked up. Gareth? Gareth was dead. How could he possibly envy him?

"And Gareth because, even in death, his life is more fulfilling than mine. He was always the heart of the vampire community through his good deeds and his bravery. I wish I could be more like him."

I knew I shouldn't eavesdrop on such a private conversation, but I was riveted. In his confession, Dante had just demonstrated that he had more heart than he even recognized.

"Number four. I used several swear words after noticing another five pounds on the scale. I shall do ten Hail Marys in penance."

As he began to recite the prayer, I slipped out of the pew and made my way to the exit. Thankfully, the door was still open. I didn't want Dante to know anyone had been listening. Well, I wanted him to believe someone was listening, just not me. I was pretty sure the whole point of talking to God was that he hoped He was listening. It was a nice thought. I only wished I believed it.

I fled the church and returned to the academy classroom, slamming the door behind me to make my entrance obvious.

"Perfect timing," Professor Holmes said. "We've just reconvened to talk about the results of our brief investigation."

My elation was short-lived as the results were uneventful.

"Well, the good news is I unearthed a lot of great information today," I announced. And some devastating information, too.

Professor Holmes looked at the other girls. "Do you think she's talking? Emma, do you remember that we can't hear you?"

Crap.

He slid over a quill and parchment. Time for another hand cramp. I wish there was a Google translator for invisible people. I wrote down the important details of my day, omitting the part about Daniel as well as Dante's minor confessions.

The professor skimmed my note. "A missing grimoire from Josef's house?" He gave his chin a thoughtful stroke. "Yes, of course."

Millie read over his shoulder. "Did the coven know about Josef's collection of books?" She glanced at the kindly professor. "I can't imagine Lady Weatherby allowing it."

Professor Holmes nodded. "Quite right, Millie. Josef was an old and accomplished wizard. He kept the books a secret from the coven. We had every intention of securing them once his estate was settled. There was apparently a delay with the paperwork. I don't know the particulars."

Millie brightened. "When we went to the registrar's office, there was a deed and a will for Josef filed on the date the spell took hold."

"The deed to the house and the will?" Professor Holmes queried. "That is odd."

Not odd if Felix was the one who cast the spell.

"Do we know if Josef intended to leave his house to Felix?" Sophie asked. "We assumed so because he's Josef's only living relative, but what if he didn't?"

They were on a roll. If Josef didn't leave his house to Felix in the will, the one way to fix it after Josef's death would be to go to the registrar's office and try to swap out the existing documents.

"Emma was right," Sophie said. "The spell probably wasn't meant for the council. It was meant for Stan."

"To distract him so that Felix could change the documents," Begonia added.

"Are you listening, Emma?" Millie asked the empty air.

I wrote down that I was and that I'd check Felix's house for the grimoire.

"That doesn't seem wise," Professor Holmes said. "Felix is likely the one who made you invisible. He must have known you were on his trail. That puts you in danger."

"Let's ask Astrid to see if she can head over to his place," Begonia said.

"And bypass the sheriff entirely?" Professor Holmes asked. "I don't know…"

"Have you met Sheriff Hugo?" Millie asked, her tongue acid.

The professor bowed his head. "Yes, I take your point. Let's send Astrid over. She may need a search warrant if he refuses to cooperate. That could take time."

"How much time do we have?" Sophie asked. "Didn't you say…?" She trailed off and tossed a guilty glance in my general direction.

I knew there was something they hadn't told me yet.

The professor sighed softly. "Emma, you should also know that I have been looking into various invisibility spells and, I have to tell you, it's not good news. I know we're focused on reversing the youth spell, but if we don't reverse your spell soon as well, there is a risk that you will simply fade away."

I gaped at him. Fade away? I scribbled another note.

"It seems that the longer you are invisible, the more you risk losing your connection to the physical realm," he explained. "We already cannot hear you or see you. Eventually, this isolation will drive a wedge between you and the physical world. A permanent wedge."

Spell's bells. So I'd become an undead ghost?

Begonia gasped. "We have to get her back."

"If our theory about Felix is correct, it is likely both spells can be found in the missing grimoire," Professor Holmes said. "The sooner we get ours hands on it, the sooner we can reverse them both."

I nodded vigorously, not that anyone could see me.

"So what do we do?" Millie asked. "Wait for Astrid?"

"I'll go and see her now," Professor Holmes said. "Until she can speak with him and determine whether the grimoire is in his possession, I recommend we simply wait."

Easy for him to say. He wasn't on the verge of fading into oblivion.

I was terrible at waiting. I paced around my house like a caged werelion, driving Sedgwick out of his tiny bird brain.

If you don't stop, I'm going to hide a mouse in your sheets tonight.

"You hide a mouse in my sheets and that will be the last mouse you ever see," I shot back.

You're feisty when you're impatient.

Gareth swept into the room, surprised to see me. "What are you doing here?"

I stared blankly at him. "It's my house. Why wouldn't I be here?"

"Isn't tonight the party hosted by Markos?" he asked.

I smacked my forehead, forgetting all about the minotaur's invitation. Oh well. What did it matter now? I was hardly in a position to attend a party.

"I'm invisible, Gareth," I pointed out. "Not much point in

attending a party." Not to mention I was downright miserable.

"Are you mad? You're living my dream right now," he said. "Do you know much I wish I could haunt a party? I don't care if no one can see me. I can see them and enjoy the festive atmosphere."

You should go, Sedgwick chimed in. *You're doing nothing here except annoying me.*

What else is new?

"Look on the bright side," Gareth said. "Now you can leave the house the way you normally do and I won't criticize you for it."

I rolled my eyes. "Fine, I'll go." If for no other reason than to enjoy the company of new people, even if they couldn't enjoy mine.

Once I arrived at the party, I felt a rise of excitement. As inconvenient as invisibility was, I admit I took a little pleasure in the freedom. Gareth was right, it didn't matter how I looked. Mismatched socks, frizzy hair—I had no one to impress when invisible. In fact, I changed into pajamas before I left the house so that I could get straight into bed when I got home. Bonus.

Despite our focus on Felix, I planned to watch people interact when they didn't know anyone was looking and listen for clues. A relaxed social situation like this one was the perfect opportunity to find out if anyone had information about the spells or even just the missing grimoire. It was also an opportunity to observe Markos and decide for myself if I had any interest. With Daniel doing who-knows-what with Elsa, I had to force myself to consider other options, however difficult it was to digest.

I maneuvered through the guests, picking up bits and

pieces of conversation. The music was great—Markos had hired Look Mom, No Wings. I'd heard them play at Moonshine with Demetrius and they were very good. I recognized a number of faces, including Ginger and a few other witches. I was surprised to see Calliope and Freya Minor there. Although people seemed to enjoy their company, the two youngest harpies were rarely seen in mixed social situations. I prayed that they didn't learn their dance moves from their Aunt Phoebe. The older harpy's dance moves bordered on obscene.

I noticed that the guests skewed heavily toward estrogen. Attractive estrogen. I wondered if Markos was determined to keep competition at a minimum. As I watched him mingle with the crowd, he seemed like a good host, chatting with one group for a reasonable time and then moving on to dance with another group. His moves were impressive. He was naturally sexy—a friendly guy having a good time.

The tempo picked up and more guests began to dance. I started tapping my foot to the music and pretty soon I was in full-blown dance mode. I couldn't remember the last time I'd really let loose and danced. I was literally dancing like no one was watching—because no one was. I tossed my hair around, threw my arms in the air, and wiggled my bottom like I was a backup dancer for Beyoncé. It was liberating.

Then my heart stopped, along with my twerk.

Daniel strolled into the room with Elsa on his arm. The thing that struck me wasn't his presence—although that was unexpected—it was the smile on his face as he greeted people. He was in the thick of the crowd, talking and shaking hands. He appeared at ease and…content. As much as it pained me to see him with someone else, I dearly loved seeing that thousand-watt smile.

"No sign of the new witch, huh?" I heard someone say. I turned around to see a troll talking to Markos.

"Sadly, no," Markos replied. "I was really hoping to get to know her tonight. Do you think I should have delivered the invitation in person?" He looked thoughtful. "I sent the owl because I didn't want her to feel obligated to say yes."

"You made the right call," the troll said. "Maybe it has something to do with the town council. I heard she's been busy following up leads."

"I suppose it's possible," Markos said, his disappointment evident.

"Well, you look fabulous," the troll said, straightening the minotaur's bow tie. It was an impressive feat that Markos managed to make a bow tie look sexy.

"Thanks, Trent." He surveyed the room. "At least everyone seems to be having a good time. It's a nice distraction from the mayhem in town right now."

"I saw Daniel Starr. Did you invite him?" Trent asked. "That doesn't seem like you."

Markos chuckled. "No, I invited Elsa and Jasper, but it seems there's been a regime change."

"Good for you, though, right?" Trent asked. "Weren't people speculating about Daniel and the witch?"

"Emma," Markos corrected him. "Her name is Emma, not 'the witch.'"

"Right, sorry." The troll turned pink. "I meant no disrespect."

Markos clapped him on the shoulder. "I know. Do me a favor and let me know if you see her."

"There are so many people here," Trent said. "You could easily miss her."

"No," Markos said, his gaze sweeping the room one more time. "I couldn't miss *her*. She has a presence, you know what I mean?"

"I haven't met her, so I'll take your word for it." He peered around the minotaur to where two pixies were dancing, their bodies pressed close together. "Have fun. I'm going to make myself a pixie sandwich."

I continued to watch Markos for another minute as he observed his guests. There was something appealing about him, although I wasn't sure how I'd feel about his true minotaur form. The horns and the fur might be a real turnoff for me.

Markos moved toward the bar and I was left alone in the middle of the crowd. My earlier euphoria was replaced by what could only be described as melancholy. I watched the guests dancing, drinking, and otherwise enjoying themselves. They were all part of this moment and I was with them, yet painfully apart from them. No one could see me or hear me. I hadn't felt this alone since my grandmother's death. After she died, I remembered going through the motions of life—going to work, food shopping, doing laundry in the basement—but I didn't feel connected to anything or anyone around me.

My gaze fell upon Daniel. Elsa's head rested against his chest as they swayed to the music. In my moment of despair and isolation, I understood him more than I ever had before. The way I felt right now—this must be the reason he'd made the decision to reunite with Elsa. He'd been trying to earn his redemption to ease his suffering, but good deeds by themselves wouldn't be enough to quell the hole in his heart. He needed to feel that connection to another living being. It was the whole package he wanted. Not just life but a reason to live.

I swallowed the lump in my throat. Even though I understood his decision to seek a romantic connection, why couldn't he have chosen me? After all, we had a deep connection—or so I believed. Then again, he and Elsa had a history that I knew very little about. She'd loved him once, which already made her the safer bet. Maybe I was simply a risk he wasn't willing to take.

A pixie flew into me, nearly knocking me to the ground.

The pixie looked at her friend. "Who put that wall there?" She laughed loudly, spilling her drink all over the floor.

I began to push my way through the crowd. My face felt hot and I was desperate for air. Professor Holmes was right. Invisibility was not good in the long run. I needed to break the spell and soon.

I barged out of the house and tumbled into the quiet darkness. Dozens of stars winked at me from above, refusing to share their secrets.

One fateful day I was on my way to meet a client in the Poconos and now I was escaping a minotaur's party—a party apparently designed to make my acquaintance. How did I end up in Spellbound? How was I—Emma Hart from Lemon Grove, Pennsylvania—a wicked sorceress parading around a paranormal town as a witch? It all seemed like an insane dream.

You look ready to go home, Sedgwick said.

I glanced upward. "What are you doing here?"

Just passing by and saw you.

"Liar."

Don't leave your glass slipper behind. I don't need anyone knocking on the door at ungodly hours.

The only thing glass is me, I replied. I was, it seemed, transparent and entirely breakable.

Did you learn anything useful? he asked.

"Yes and no." I didn't have the heart to elaborate. I glanced skyward again and noticed his silhouette directly above me. "To the right, please."

He sighed loudly. *If nothing else, you're consistent.*

CHAPTER 17

Astrid dropped by the house the next day to report that Felix's house had provided no clues.

"I'm sorry, Emma," she said. "I've been hoping to solve this case, but it's been one roadblock after another."

We stood in what used to be Gareth's old home office, where I wrote my responses to Astrid on his parchment.

"If it's any consolation, I think you're right about Felix," she said. "His reaction to my presence was shady, to say the least. He went out as soon as I left, so I tailed him to the town square. Looked like he was headed to Broomstix. I'm going to speak with the sheriff now about bringing him in for questioning."

That was good news. If anyone could break him in an interrogation, it was the tough Valkyrie.

I scribbled a note of thanks, and waited for her to leave before heading out the door.

"Where do you think you're going, missy?" Gareth asked.

I knew there was one more place to look for the grimoire.

"Into town," I said, adopting my breeziest tone. "Do you need anything?"

"A little flesh and bone would be nice," he said. "See if you can pick some up at the Wish Market."

"You're hilarious," I said.

Gareth observed me. "You have a glint in your eye that spells trouble. What are you planning to do?"

"Nothing," I replied, and hurried out the door before he could stop me.

I found his car easily, parked in front of Broomstix. It didn't surprise me to discover it was unlocked. Spellbound residents weren't overly concerned with crime. I waited until no one was watching and popped open the side door. Just because I was invisible didn't mean no one would notice a door opening on its own.

I started with the glove compartment and found nothing except a pile of crumpled napkins and a few coffee-stained cup stoppers. Felix was a bit of a slob, apparently. How unlike his meticulous father.

I climbed into the backseat and checked behind and under the driver and passenger seats. Nothing there. There was no real trunk space to speak of given that the jalopies here were closer to Ford Model-T's than modern cars. My 1988 green Volvo was an exception because it had come from the human world and been magically enhanced by Quinty, a handy elf.

As I was about to leave, the driver's door opened and Felix got behind the wheel. I cringed. Now what? There was no time to escape. He pulled away from the curb and I sat in the seat behind him, praying I didn't suddenly become visible again. That would be just my luck.

Sedgwick, I cried as loudly as I could in my head. *Great balls of a minotaur, I need help! Sedgwick, follow Felix's car.* I really needed to figure out the extent of our telepathic range. Was it better than a Verizon signal?

To my surprise, Felix didn't drive in the direction of his house. After a few minutes, I recognized the passing landscape. We were going to Josef's—to his father's house. Was he simply going to pack up the contents of the house? Or was he going to return the grimoire, knowing that Astrid was looking for it? There was only one way to know for sure.

I gathered my courage and waited patiently for Felix to park the car and go inside. I noticed that he entered the house empty-handed. No book.

He's inside the house, Sedgwick's voice thundered, and I nearly hit my head on the ceiling of the car.

I'm invisible, not blind, I said. *But I'm so glad you're here. I wasn't sure if you could hear me.*

You scared the mouse right out of my mouth, but I'll try not to hold it against you in light of the kidnapping.

Technically, it's not kidnapping since I got in the car voluntarily and he doesn't know I'm here.

Sedgwick groaned. *Always with the technicalities. You'd think you were a lawyer.*

I opened the car door as slowly as possible and crept to the front door. *I don't suppose you can see where he is in the house.*

I have night vision, not X-ray vision, he said. *Get a move on. If the book is in there, you need to strike while the sword is sharp.*

Stay here in case I need help, I said, although I wasn't entirely sure how Sedgwick could fend off a wizard.

I cracked open the door and looked around before stepping inside. There was no sign of Felix. Off to the right, the sound of footsteps stopped me in my tracks. I held my breath and waited. When the sound finally faded, I moved again. I passed the display of crystals and headed straight upstairs to the library.

Despite my instincts, I was surprised to see the grimoire back on the stand. I suppose I hadn't completely accepted that Felix was to blame. That maybe there was another explanation.

I began to turn the pages, frantically looking for the relevant spells.

"Come out, come out, wherever you are," he called.

Uh oh. How did he know I was here?

I stared at the grimoire. I couldn't take it with me because a floating book would give my location away. I'd have to leave it for now. Felix was smart to return it to his father's home. They wouldn't be able to tie the spell to him. Lots of people were in and out of the wizard's house during the wake. Any one of them could have looked up the spell or taken the book during that time. The house had been open to everyone in town.

"Let's not drag this out, Miss Hart," he said. "I know you figured me out. That seems to be your special skill. If I had been smarter, I would have made sure you were already in the building at the critical time when I cast the spell."

I padded across the room, looking for something to use as a weapon.

"There is no escape," he said. "I've warded every door in the house. You won't be able to leave here alive. I am sorry for that. You're new to town and people seem to like you. A shame."

Not everyone, I thought glumly. Not in the way I wanted. It was unsurprising that my final thoughts would be of Daniel. He was probably with Elsa right now, lavishing her with affection. I had so hoped that it would be me one day. If Felix had his way, no one would ever have the chance to fall in love with me. I would die the way I'd lived in the human world. Alone.

I heard his footsteps approaching and moved to the other

side of a bookcase. His attention went straight to the open grimoire and he crossed the room to inspect it.

"I see you've been thumbing through here. Did you know I used the same invisibility spell on the grimoire as I used on you?" He laughed heartily. "Took it out of my house right under Astrid's nose and brought it in here right under yours. Clever, huh?"

There was no point in replying since he couldn't hear me.

"I suppose you were looking for the reversal spell, you naive girl. Do you think I'd be so foolish as to leave it in? I removed that page. I am not the lackluster wizard my father believed me to be."

No, Felix had proven himself to be far from lackluster.

Felix stood in front of the grimoire. "And now it is time for another spell. I've been getting quite adept since my father died. I do believe some of his power may have transferred to me during the funeral ritual. It has been known to happen on occasion."

Another spell? Which one did he plan to do now?

"I'm sure you're eager to find out what I have planned," he said. "I'm now going to turn you visible again." He removed a folded piece of parchment from his pocket and placed it on the open grimoire. "You can hide, but it's only a waste of time. I will find you in due time. Although it is a grand house, it's not so large that the predator cannot find its prey."

"You don't have to do this, Felix," I said, knowing he couldn't hear me. "It was just a youth spell. You didn't kill anyone." Yet.

He squinted over the paper. "How I do love the sound of Latin. It saddens me that the coven no longer favors it."

It didn't sadden me. I had enough time performing spells in English. Latin would be my undoing.

As he began to recite the spell, I dashed through the open doorway and down the steps. I needed to get as far away from him as possible before I turned visible. If the house was warded, then I needed to bide my time and hope the cavalry arrived, not that anyone was expected. Maybe Sedgwick would come through for me, not that he would be able to communicate with anyone else. The most he could do was annoy someone to the point of following him. To be fair, that often worked.

I traveled down another flight of stairs and into the cellar. It wasn't like the cellar in my home that Gareth had designed as his master bedroom. This was a true cellar, with dismal walls and a damp smell. It was the kind of cellar you expected someone to be tortured in. I shivered. I had to banish negative thoughts. I wasn't going to survive if I let my fears take over.

I should have brought my wand. When would I learn to never leave it behind? Then again, it seemed that only my clothing was invisible along with my body. Anything else would have given me away.

Across the room, I spotted another set of stairs that appeared to lead to the outside. What if he neglected to ward all of the doors? What if he only did the obvious ones? It was a large house. He could have missed a set.

I bolted for the rickety wooden steps and tried to push my way through the storm doors. They refused to budge. I couldn't tell whether it was because of magic or because of the weight of heavy-duty steel. I tried again, using all of my strength to push the doors open and was rewarded with a sharp pain in my shoulder blade.

Okay, if brute strength wasn't going to work, then I had to think like a witch. I knew from experience that I didn't necessarily need a wand to perform magic. Then the words of the Grey sisters flashed in my mind. I wasn't even an ordinary witch. According to them, I was a starlight sorceress. Dark magic resided in me—in my blood and in my bones.

What would happen if I tried to access it? The mere thought frightened me. What if I conjured up something awful? What if the magic changed me or opened a door within me that I could never close again? I had to take the risk. If I didn't try, I would be dead within the hour.

I closed my eyes and cleared my thoughts. I had no idea how to access the darkness within me. More than that—what if the Grey sisters were wrong? Now was not the time to discover I was the remedial witch everyone else believed me to be.

A blast of air went through me and I knew Felix had completed the spell. I was visible again. The only good news was that Felix was still upstairs, probably going room by room to find me. If he believed there was no escape, then he wouldn't rush. I wondered how he intended to explain my death in his father's house. He probably would pretend to be the one to find me. What a jerk.

I focused my will the way Lady Weatherby had taught me. I decided to try the Blowback spell first. Although it was meant for another person, maybe it would work on a set of doors.

"Step on a crack/suffer blowback."

I flew backward, landing squarely on my bottom. One bruised tailbone coming up. I stood on shaky legs and concentrated again. This was a life or death situation. If I didn't find a way to open those doors, then I would die in this horrible cellar. Daniel would never know how I felt about him. For whatever reason, that fact bothered me more than anything else. It didn't matter that he didn't return my feelings. It only mattered that he was in the world, doing his good deeds and seeking redemption. I wanted his halo restored whether I was a part of his life or not.

Tears stung my eyes and I straightened my shoulders. I wasn't ready to give up yet. Instead, I dug in. I didn't know how to access the darkness within me, but I did know how to access the light. The love. I pulled every strong memory to the forefront. My sweet mother and her tender hugs. My father and his valiant attempt to rebuild our lives after her death. My grandparents who struggled to raise me. I even thought of Huey, my stuffed owl. The way he smelled. The way he felt, soft and loving.

Huey.

In that moment, I realized that I'd been wrong about Huey. We'd mistakenly believed the toy owl was a clue to my origin—a link to my coven—but it wasn't really. I had no doubt that Huey was the reason Sedgwick and I chose each other. It was my love for Huey that summoned the spotted owl and it was my power that drew him to me. It was an unnerving and exciting revelation.

"Come out, Emma. I have important matters to attend to."

His voice echoed before I heard his footsteps above my head. He was coming.

I took a long, deep breath and summoned every ounce of power in my body. There was no time for a rhyming spell. I simply threw out my hands and released a primal scream. It wasn't the piercing kind that female victims often had in horror films. It was a gut-wrenching scream, the kind that if you'd heard it, you'd weep for the source of the sound. It began in the deepest part of my soul and rumbled from my body in painful, soul-crushing waves. The doors not only blew open, they blew straight off the hinges.

There was no time to stop and wonder at what I'd just done. The longer I lingered, the more likely it was that I wouldn't make it out of the cellar alive.

CHAPTER 18

THANKS to the explosion of power, I was now too weak to move. Instead of running outside like I'd planned, I dropped to my knees and my palms slammed against the concrete floor.

"How in Mother Nature's name...?" Felix stood on the stairs, frozen in disbelief. "You're nothing but a remedial witch. How could you possibly have broken through my ward?"

I didn't wait to answer him. I gathered my strength and crawled up the wooden steps and into the darkness. I didn't have much of a lead, but it would be harder for him to find me out here. I stumbled to my feet and ran. There were plenty of trees to climb or hide behind. I debated whether to climb the sturdy oak I saw up ahead. No, I was too weak to climb. Besides, it would have been just another trap. He would simply stand at the base of it until I came down or use his magic to break the branch I was on. Or, if he grew impatient, he'd simply light a match and burn it down. No, I had to keep running. There were neighbors, albeit not too close. Maybe I had a chance.

"Give up, Emma," he yelled. "You've lost. I have proven myself a great wizard and you are nothing more than a remedial witch." Again with the putdown. So he wasn't just a psychopath, he was a sexist psychopath. I wasn't sure which one bothered me more. It was then that I caught a glimpse of a shadow circling the air above my head.

Sedgwick, is that you? I had never hoped more to see my familiar. For a moment, there was no response and I began to doubt my vision, but then—

What's happening down there? Sedgwick asked. *You're visible again, but why are you running?*

I choked back tears. *Sedgwick,* I cried. *You beautiful gift of an owl.*

You're delirious, he said. *Has he poisoned you?*

Felix is trying to kill me. I just used a bucket load of magic and I'm too weak to fight him off.

Say no more, Your Highness, he replied.

I didn't know what Sedgwick could do to help me. Somehow, I doubted pooping on Felix's head would be enough to save me. Hopefully, the owl had another weapon in his arsenal.

Just to be clear, did I hear you say 'great balls of a minotaur' earlier?

Sedgwick, I'm sort of in the middle of an emergency right now, I said. *Can we not worry about expressions I blurt out in times of extreme stress?*

No need to be embarrassed. It just means you're starting to fit in.

I thought about my feelings of isolation during Markos's party. Was I truly fitting in here?

I felt fingers encircle my ankle and, before I could scream, Felix tackled me to the ground. The wizard moved like a panther. I didn't even hear him approach.

He straddled me, holding a wand in his fist and raising it above my chest like he was about to stake me with it.

"I learned this spell in wizard camp and never got the chance to use it," he said, his eyes ablaze with power and aggression.

As he opened his mouth for the incantation, Sedgwick swooped down and snatched the wand from his grasp. Felix glanced up in surprise and the owl unloaded his next trick.

"Ugh, my eye," Felix cried, smearing the poop to his temple.

It was enough of a distraction to allow me to punch him in the groin and push him aside. He grunted and doubled over.

What spell was that? Sedgwick asked, observing Felix's discomfort from the air.

No spell. Just good, old-fashioned self-defense.

I scrambled to my feet as Felix recovered.

"Release my wand, you foul creature," he bellowed.

That's f-o-w-l to you, Sedgwick taunted, not that Felix could hear him.

Felix advanced toward me, a murderous glint in his eye. I was still too drained to summon any magic.

"Stop right there, Felix," a voice boomed.

Felix scowled at the figure behind me. I turned around to see Professor Holmes, his wand extended, flanked by Sheriff Hugo and Astrid.

"Drop your wand," Sheriff Hugo ordered.

Felix glanced skyward as Sedgwick glided toward the sheriff and dropped the wand at the centaur's hooves. I ran over and plucked the wand off the ground, pointing it at Felix. Despite the presence of this powerful trio, I didn't want to take any chances.

"Disarm her," Felix said. "Don't let her use magic on me."

Astrid sauntered over to him, twirling a pair of magic

handcuffs. "Cut the act, Felix. You were the one who was about to kill her. You didn't look too scared when you had her pinned to the ground."

"She didn't have a wand then," he said.

Professor Holmes chuckled. "It's nice to know our witches have a solid reputation."

"You don't understand," Felix sputtered. "She broke through my ward. That's impossible."

Little did he realize I didn't have a wand then either.

"Impossible indeed," Professor Holmes said. "I have no doubt that you failed to ward them all properly. Perhaps, in your haste, you missed one. It wouldn't surprise me. You never were a very good student."

"I don't think I did," he murmured, more to himself. "I was so careful. Always so careful. It was why I was so angry with my father for not leaving the house to me."

"And you found the spell in one of your father's grimoires?" the sheriff asked.

"It fell on the floor when I was cleaning up after the wake and it opened to the page with the youth spell," Felix explained. "It was kismet."

"Not quite," I said.

"All of his wonderful books and artifacts," Felix continued. "I was his only living heir, but he wanted to donate his entire estate to that wretched animal rescue center! Like I wasn't a wizard worthy of the inheritance."

"I'm afraid you won't be seeing this house again for quite some time," Sheriff Hugo said. "Attempted murder and casting a dangerous spell on the town council will cost you dearly."

"Don't forget the invisibility spell on Emma," Professor Holmes said.

Felix soured and jabbed a finger in my direction. "You

need to keep an eye on that girl. Something isn't right with her. Don't you feel it?"

"Sounds like a case of sour burstberries to me," Astrid said, and pushed him forward.

I, of course, said nothing. Daniel was adamant that no one discover the truth about me and I trusted his judgment. At least on this matter.

A flash of white in the distance caught my eye. Speak of the angel and he appears. He landed with his usual grace and rushed toward me, his expression tense.

"Emma," he called. "Thank heaven, you're safe." He sounded so relieved that I nearly burst into tears.

"I am," I said. They were the only two words I could muster. He wrapped his arms around me and I felt the soft touch of his feathers brush against my skin.

"I should have suspected Felix," he said. "I never cared for him."

"No one suspected him," I said. "Not even me and I was the one who should have realized first."

"How can you say that?" he asked. "You're the newest person here. You know far less about everyone than the rest of us."

I removed myself from his embrace and gazed up at him. "If there's one thing I've learned since I came here, it's that you don't know each other as well as you think. In fact, you don't even know yourselves as well as you think." It was the closest I came to mentioning Elsa and what I knew. I wouldn't force the issue. I would wait for him to tell me when he was ready. As much as it would pain me to hear the words spoken, I needed the truth. I knew my heart would refuse to let go of the last shred of hope until it had no choice.

The worst part was that this was not Daniel the player. This was Daniel's new leaf. If he was willing to enter into a relationship with Elsa again, it was because he'd decided to commit to her. Because he chose to love her, not because he was reverting to type. That fact hurt me most of all. I had believed his new leaf would lead him directly to me. Inwardly, I scolded myself for waiting. I should have told him how I felt, even if it changed nothing. Even though I told myself in the cellar that I would tell Daniel the truth, standing before him now, I no longer had the courage. I needed his friendship more than anything. I couldn't say something that would risk losing it. And if Elsa knew, she would be sure to exclude me from his life. She didn't seem like the type of fairy who would be able to tolerate a potential rival's love for her paramour.

And what if he married her? What then? Oh no. I felt sick.

"Emma," Astrid said. "You look like you might…"

The vomit hit the ground and sprayed everyone's shoes within a two-foot radius.

"I'm sorry," I croaked. "I think it must be the aftereffects of the visibility spell." A complete lie.

Someone produced a blanket and tossed it across my shoulders. Daniel placed an arm around me and guided me away from the group. "Let me escort you home. We don't have to fly."

Ever so gently, I shook him off. "Astrid will take me," I said. I couldn't bring myself to look at him. If I gazed into those turquoise eyes, I knew my resolve would crumble.

"Astrid? Are you sure?"

"I'm sure. Thank you, Daniel. I'm sure you have better things to do than worry about me."

His expression was a mixture of pain and confusion. "Why would you say that? Of course I want to worry about you." He paused. "Wait. That came out wrong. I don't *want* to worry about you…"

I squeezed his arm. "Stay on your path, Daniel. I'm sure ours will cross again."

He frowned. "What's wrong? What's gotten into you?"

"I guess, like the town council is about to do, I'm growing up." I said, and signaled to Astrid that it was time to take me home.

As quickly as possible, we gathered the afflicted members of the council as well as the registrar and secured them in the Great Hall, the place where it all began.

I'd enlisted the aid of Linsey, the young berserker I defended in a vandalism case. She taught children in an after school art program and I knew she could handle a bunch of whiny council members.

Linsey glanced around, surprised to see the room filled with people. "What is it you want me to do?"

"I have several town council members in need of an art director for the next half an hour," I said. "I think you're the right person for the job."

"They're still under the spell?" she queried, as Lord Gilder bounced a ball off the dais.

"Hopefully not for much longer. I need someone with a firm hand to deal with them while we work on the reversal spell. I need them here, but don't want them getting in the way."

Linsey flicked her nose ring. "One tough babysitter coming right up. What should I have them do?"

"They can draw hand turkeys or throw finger paint at each other for all I care," I said. "Just keep them contained in the Great Hall and out of trouble."

A slow grin spread across her face. "Leave it to me," she said.

With the 'children' occupied, I was able to focus on the

spell with Professor Holmes and the remedial witches. Ginger and Meg were also on hand to assist. Together we reviewed the spell.

"Are we sure it's time to change them back?" Meg asked. "It's been kind of enjoyable to watch them."

Professor Holmes snatched the spell from her hand. "That's because you've spent most of the time in your aerobics studio."

I stifled a laugh. The professor definitely bore the brunt of Lady Weatherby's absence.

"I can't believe Felix was able to do a spell of this magnitude," Ginger said. "He's never shown much promise."

"He mentioned that he felt like some of his father's power was transferred to him during the funeral," I said. "Do you think it's possible?"

"Undoubtedly," Professor Holmes said. "And his father possessed that treasure trove of grimoires and other spell books. We were fortunate, really. He could have done much worse."

I glanced over my shoulder at Lorenzo, who was busy picking his nose. "Some of the council members might beg to differ."

"Let's get on with it," Ginger said. "I'm tired of keeping the peace. I want order restored now."

We held hands, forming a chain, and recited the incantation together. Professor Holmes thought that the more power we injected, the more likely the spell was to work. The incantation was more complex than the simple rhyming spells I'd learned at the academy so far and I stumbled over a few of the Latin words. Nevertheless, a spark of light indicated the completion of the spell and we watched in anticipation as the council members regained adult consciousness.

Lady Weatherby stared at her hand, which was covered in red paint. I could tell by her concerned expression that she thought it was blood. She sniffed her palm and her face relaxed.

Mayor Knightsbridge studied the artwork in front of her. She'd drawn…well, I had no idea what she'd tried to draw, but the paper was splattered with pink paint and glitter.

"What's going on?" she demanded. "Why am I elbow-deep in the middle of some elementary school art class?"

Cautiously, I approached the group. "You don't remember?"

Stan blinked. "Remember what? Why am I in here? I should be in my office. I think." He scratched his head. "What time is it?"

On the one hand, I was relieved they wouldn't remember their brief return to childhood. On the other hand, it saddened me to think that Lady Weatherby would have no memory of her visit with Agnes. I sighed. At least Agnes would remember. That would have to be enough.

"Professor Holmes," Lady Weatherby said sharply. "Explain yourself."

So he did. The council was mortified, despite the fact that he left out the more embarrassing parts of the story.

"I shall head to the town square this instant and reassure the public that I am in charge," Mayor Knightsbridge said, and fluttered straight out the door.

The rest of the group looked shell shocked, but dragged themselves out the door and to their respective homes. Only Lady Weatherby lingered. She looked down her aquiline nose at me. "I trust you enjoyed yourself immensely at our expense."

"To be honest, I didn't enjoy it at all," I said.

Lady Weatherby inclined her head. "Are you certain?"

"Okay, fine," I relented. "I enjoyed watching you kick butt in dodgeball. In your defense, you're very good at it. You might want to consider getting together an adult game. You seemed to relish pummeling your colleagues with whatever you could get your hands on."

The hint of a smile played on her lips.

"I shall take it under advisement," she said. "Anything else I need to know?"

"There are some amazing people in this town, including Professor Holmes." Despite the slide toward anarchy, there was a real team effort to keep the town functioning during the crisis.

"Thank you, Emma. That's very kind of you to say." He fidgeted with his pointy blue hat, slightly taken off guard by the compliment.

"The council thanks each and every one of you for your service," Lady Weatherby said.

I was fairly certain she'd knock me unconscious with her wand if I tried to hug her. As weird as the whole experience was, I appreciated seeing the softer, more vulnerable side of Lady Weatherby. Although she didn't often show it, I'd made an important discovery—that behind her iron cloak beat a bleeding heart.

CHAPTER 19

The next morning I went straight to Rochester's office. I knew he'd been up to his eyeballs in paperwork ever since the council reverted to childhood, but we needed to resolve the case against Russ.

"Miss Hart, what a lovely surprise," he said. "Please sit."

Initially, I wasn't a fan of the wizard, but he'd slowly won me over, especially when he expressed his support for legal reform.

"I came to talk about Russ," I said.

"The spells have been broken." He frowned. "Are you looking to delay the trial?"

"I'm not here to ask for a delay. I've come to offer a plea."

His eyebrows shot up. "A plea?"

"Russ acknowledges hitting Edgar, although he'd like us to take into account that he was aiming for Henrik."

"Henrik is mortal. His injuries could've been far worse than Edgar's."

I nodded. "Russ knows that and he's sorry. He's willing to serve time, but if you and I work out a plea arrangement, we can determine the sentencing." I gave him a knowing look.

"Miss Hart," he said with an air of approval. "You have proven yourself far more cunning than I would ever have imagined." He polished the tip of his wand with a crisp, white handkerchief. "You do realize a judge must approve the deal. It isn't a guarantee."

"I'm willing to take the gamble," I said. "I wasn't able to put my request for reform in front of the council because of the spell. Until I can get things moving, I'd like to find other ways to help my clients."

"Subversive," he murmured. "And what does Gareth think about your creative lawyering? He was always so by the book."

"You've heard about his ghost then?"

He set down his wand and smiled. "I think word has gotten around."

"Gareth is in favor of reform. In fact, I think he'd like to be a part of the commission, if the council approves the idea."

"His sharp mind would be an asset," Rochester agreed.

"Russ is a decent guy who lost his temper," I said. "He's willing to pay a price, but I think you'd agree that life in prison seems over the top. Edgar has also requested leniency. He's willing to speak with you, if necessary."

"For someone who grew up not knowing you had magic, you've certainly managed to work your magic on the people of Spellbound."

Pink colored my cheeks. I wasn't great at accepting compliments. "I care about them, Rochester. Everyone I've met is so nice and they mean well..." Okay, maybe Mike the wereweasel was a jerk, but even he didn't deserve life in prison.

"Was it like this for you back in the human world?" Rochester asked. "Did your joie de vivre permeate your every move there as well?"

I blinked. "My what?"

"Your joy for life," he said. "It radiates from you. Tell me you don't feel it. It's as sure and steady as your beating heart."

Joie de vivre. It sounded like the opposite of Daniel's outlook. No wonder we were drawn to each other. Maybe that explained his interest in me. It had never been a romantic interest—I was a lifeline. An anchor to this world, to keep him from slipping into the void.

"Thank you, Rochester," I said. "What a lovely compliment."

He shuffled the papers on his desk. "Now then. Back to business. Let's see what kind of agreement we can reach for your client, shall we?"

After my successful meeting with Rochester, I made the long drive toward Curse Cliff. I was exhausted from the events of the past week, but I needed to make good on my promise to Gareth. The Grey sister didn't make much small talk on the way back to my house. She seemed content to watch the scenery pass by. A novelty for her, living in the cave away from town.

I parked Sigmund in the driveway and turned to my visitor. "You'll need to be mindful of Magpie. He's Gareth's cat and very protective of him. If he thinks you're trying to hurt his friend, he will bleed your wrinkled body dry and leave you a husk."

"Sounds like my kind of cat."

"And don't try to eat my owl. He's not one of your chickens."

The Grey sister smiled, revealing a new set of false teeth. "You're so dramatic. Although I suppose that is typical of your kind."

"My kind being a witch," I reminded her. "A plain witch, remember? Nothing more."

"As you desire, Mistress of the Dark." Her one eye blinked innocently.

"I am not a mistress of anything." I exhaled slowly, regaining my composure. "Lyra, I need you on board. Word of advice. Don't bite the hand that feeds you a new set of chompers."

She clicked her teeth together and giggled. "My sisters are so envious. They keep trying to steal them while I'm sleeping."

No doubt.

She followed me into the house where Gareth paced the floor, anxiously awaiting our return.

"Gareth, meet your apparitional tutor, Lyra Grey," I said.

"A pleasure," he said, and attempted to shake her hand. His expression shifted to surprise when he actually made contact with her. "How did you do that?"

"Witches and fairies aren't the only ones who can make things happen," she said.

"You don't mind if I go, do you? I need to get back to the office," I said.

Gareth shot me a look of pure panic.

"I'll be back in two hours to drive you home," I told Lyra. "Try not to get in any trouble while I'm gone."

"If the house is still standing, I'll consider it a success," Lyra said. She glanced around the foyer. "I must say, it feels good to be standing in a house, although this place is almost as drafty as the cave."

"Hey," Gareth began to protest, but quickly thought better of it.

"Come along, Junior," Lyra said. "Get started we shall. After this, there's a venison steak with my name on it and I do not intend to share a single bite." She flashed her pearly whites at Gareth and he tried in vain to disguise his horror.

"Have fun, you two," I called, wriggling my fingers.

On my way through town, I noticed the line outside the registrar's office. It seemed there was a backlog for the elf to tackle thanks to Felix's spell.

I opened the door to my office and was shocked to see Mayor Knightsbridge fluttering around inside. Her starry wand hovered over one of my plants.

"Althea doesn't like people messing with her plants," I warned.

Mayor Knightsbridge snatched back her wand, mildly embarrassed. "I wouldn't want to aggravate a Gorgon now, would I?"

"How can I help you, Madame Mayor?" I seated myself at my desk.

"I understand you were instrumental in reversing the spell," she said. She continued to flutter around the room, too energetic to sit still.

"It was a team effort," I said. I was uncomfortable taking too much credit.

"Nevertheless, I'd like to award you with a key to the town," the mayor said. "The council insists. We'll hold a ceremony at the mansion. You can choose the flavor of fairy cake you'd like for the reception."

Yum. Cake. She had my full attention now.

"There is another matter," she said, and fluttered closer to my desk. "Sheriff Hugo and I are longtime friends. I have no desire to humiliate him."

I could hear the 'but' coming a mile away. "You're unhappy with his performance?"

"To put it mildly," she said, kneading her hands. "I've heard the whispers, dear. I know residents don't feel his heart is in his duties anymore, but I expected him to be the one to root out the spell caster in this case." Her eyes flashed angrily. "I was reduced to a child for heaven's sake. And where was my trusted sheriff? On the golf course? Getting a massage at Glow?"

"He did care, Madame Mayor," I said. I wasn't sure why I rose to his defense. I couldn't help myself. "He was deeply unhappy about the situation."

"Then why are *you* the one who handled it?"

I couldn't answer that. "Have you spoken with him about it?"

She pursed her lips. "There's no point. I've decided to take other measures."

My radar pinged. "What kind of measures?"

"I plan to put him in timeout," she said. "Let's see how the sheriff enjoys a long vacation."

"How long?"

"As long as I deem necessary," she said. "Astrid will be a fine interim sheriff, wouldn't you agree?"

I cleared my throat, still in shock. "Yes, one hundred percent."

"Excellent. I was hoping you would approve."

She continued to hover and I sensed one more question coming.

"I understand you've met my daughter, Elsa."

Oh boy.

"Yes, I did. Daniel and I ran into her recently." I left out the part where I snuck into her house while invisible since I was fairly certain I broke some kind of law. I braced myself for the next sentence.

"By any chance, did she mention her engagement to Jasper?"

"No." I omitted seeing the marriage license in the registrar's office since I wasn't supposed to be there either. "Is she engaged?"

"Someone said they saw her wearing a ring," the mayor

said, "but I asked Jasper about it and he looked completely blindsided. Said they'd broken up."

A tight knot formed in the pit of my stomach. "Did you ask Elsa?"

"When I find her, I will. I'm concerned she's gone and done something stupid." She gave me a knowing look. "I should think you'd be concerned as well."

I forced my mouth to work. "I can't imagine…" A world where Daniel was engaged to marry someone else.

"Let me know if you hear anything, will you? I'll have Lucy send the details to you about the ceremony for the key."

At the mention of Daniel and Elsa, I'd forgotten all about the key. "Thank you, Madame Mayor. It's a great honor."

She leaned forward and patted my hand. "Don't fret, dear. If there's a way to stop this train wreck from roaring through town, you and I are perfectly positioned to manage it."

I didn't respond. What could I say? If Daniel decided to rekindle his love for Elsa and didn't want to waste another day, what could I do?

I waited until I heard the click of the door to fall apart. Naturally, Althea chose that moment to enter my office with her watering can. I failed to hear the hiss of her snakes over my loud sobs.

"Emma?"

I jerked my head up. Fluids poured out of my eyes and nose and there was even a bit of drool out of my mouth. Althea pulled a clean tissue from her pocket and handed it to me.

"Is this about Daniel and Elsa?"

"Does everyone know except me?" How could he not tell me something so important?

"I heard about it in Brew-Ha-Ha when I stopped for a coffee break," she said. "People are excited. They think he's turned over a new leaf. He's never proposed to anyone before."

I couldn't focus. My head was dizzy and my eyes were blurry. "I can't believe this is happening."

"You should talk to him," Althea said.

I wasn't sure if I could handle a conversation with Daniel. The last thing I wanted to do was break down in front of him and embarrass myself.

"I think I need to head home," I said.

"You go ahead. I'll lock up here." She handed me a fistful of tissues.

My legs wobbled as I stood. At least I'd driven to town. I was pretty sure my legs would give out before I made it home.

As I opened Sigmund's door, I heard my name. I tried to pretend I didn't hear him and slipped into the driver's seat, but he opened the passenger door and sat beside me, his wings squashed against the seat.

"There you are," Daniel said. "I've been looking everywhere for you."

"I was in my office," I said. "You didn't try there." I couldn't bring myself to look at him. I kept my eyes focused in front of me. "What do you need?"

"Need?" he repeated. "Nothing. I wanted to share my news with you."

"If you're talking about Elsa Knightsbridge, then I've already heard."

"Oh." His broad shoulders slumped. "That's too bad. I wanted to be the one to tell you."

I blinked back tears. "How did this happen? I thought you'd sworn off the opposite sex."

"I know, but when I saw Elsa again, I remembered the good times we'd had together. And once we're married, then I'll be demonstrating commitment. True commitment."

"Do you love her?" The words burned my tongue.

"What's not to love?" he asked, and the answer was like a knife in my gut. "She's beautiful, outspoken, smart."

"You said she was spoiled."

"I also said it was one of the qualities I liked about her." He paused. "Are you angry?"

"Why would I be angry?" I asked, too quickly.

"Because I didn't tell you first."

I wanted to grab his nonexistent halo and wring his neck with it. How could he not know the way I felt about him? Did I hide it that well? Other people seemed to know. Why was he so oblivious?

"I admit that I'm surprised and disappointed…that you didn't come to me sooner. That I heard from someone else." I forced myself to look at him. "I thought we were better friends than that."

He placed his hand over mine. "We are and I'm sorry."

I knew he meant it, but it didn't matter. He'd never be as sorry as I was.

"You won't tell her about me, will you?" I asked in a hushed tone. "My secret?" Now that Daniel's loyalties were divided, the secret of my origin suddenly seemed vulnerable to discovery.

"Never," he said firmly. "I would never betray you, Emma. You should know that."

Although I nodded, my insides were screaming. As far as I was concerned, he already had.

CHAPTER 20

I WAS ABOUT to leave the house when I walked straight into a bouquet of flowers.

"Oh," I exclaimed, pulling a stray petal from my mouth.

The flowers moved aside to reveal Markos in his human form. "Sorry about that. The bouquet was bigger than I realized. I couldn't see past it."

"Are they for me?" I asked.

"A sort of Welcome Back to Visibility and Thank You for Saving the Town gesture," he said.

I took the flowers and inhaled their wonderful scent. "These are lovely, Markos. Thank you. Listen, I'm sorry about missing your party." A small but necessary lie.

"Totally understandable." He smiled, a bit unsure of himself. "I heard you were very brave, standing up to Felix."

"I was scared out of my mind," I admitted.

"And that's what makes it brave," he said. "If you weren't scared, then you'd be stupid and I don't date stupid women." He cleared his throat. "Right. I'm getting ahead of myself. Emma, I came by to ask you on a date. That is, if you're interested."

His earnest expression won me over. Those soft amber eyes alone were enough to transfix a girl.

"That would be really nice," I replied. "But maybe we could just call it a friendly outing or something? I feel like the word date has expectations attached to it and, to be honest, my life feels too complicated for expectations."

Markos sighed with relief. "That's all it is then. Two strangers getting to know each other."

I pushed aside all thoughts of Daniel. If he didn't consider me worthy of his affection, then I had no choice but to move forward.

"Then count me in."

I watched Markos leave with a spring in his step, a far cry from the brooding angel's languid walk. Hurriedly, I returned to the house to put the flowers in water.

"Another admirer, eh?" Gareth asked.

"Another new friend," I corrected him. I pulled a vase from the cupboard and filled it with water. "You like Markos, right?"

"Aye. He's a fine chap. Smart, terrific personality, body to die for." He sighed longingly. "Oh, to be alive again."

I set the vase on the windowsill in the kitchen. "You won't be alive, but maybe you'll be less ghostly once you spend enough time with Lyra."

"She's trying to show me how to exert my will on objects," he explained. "It seems my will is part of my consciousness that still exists, even without my physical body."

"Sounds complex. Let me know how it pans out."

I felt light pressure between my shoulder blades. "I can let you know right now," he said.

"Gareth, are you giving me an affectionate pat on the back?"

"Trying to."

"That's incredible," I said. "Pretty soon you'll be able to

move pots and pans. It would be difficult, but you might even be able to persuade me to let you cook." I gave him a big smile.

He folded his arms. "I've come to quite enjoy watching you muck it up. It's my daily dose of entertainment."

I scowled. "Go easy on me. I threw your deranged cat a pawty, remember?"

He groaned. "Firstly, Magpie is not deranged. He's just misunderstood. Secondly, if I ever hear you say the word 'pawty' again, there is every chance my affectionate pat may turn violent."

I laughed. "It's hard to take you seriously when you're practically transparent."

"Says the invisible girl."

The invisible girl. No, I refused to accept that role. I wanted to be a part of Spellbound. I wanted to have meaningful relationships with the other residents. To know them and care about them. I wanted to build bridges, not sequester myself on a metaphorical island.

"No, Gareth. Not invisible," I said. Invisibility was a sad and lonely place—a place I had no desire to be ever again. "I'm happy to report that Emma Hart is present and accounted for."

* * *

Thank you for reading *Lucky Charm*! If you enjoyed it, please help other readers find this book ~

1. Write a review and post it on Amazon.
2. Sign up for my new releases via e-mail here
http://eepurl.com/ctYNzf

or like me on Facebook so you can find out about the next book before it's even available.

3. Look out for *Better Than Hex*, the next book in the series!

Printed in Great Britain
by Amazon